This book has been donated by
the Friend of the Lake County Library
in recognition of the reading
achievement of

SAMANTHA NUGENT
during the teen 2012

OWN the NIGHT

Teen Summer Library Program

D0054081

Teaspoon
Detectives

Teaspoon
Detectives

THE
CASE
OF THE
MISSING
DEED

ELLEN SCHWARTZ

TUNDRA BOOKS

Text copyright © 2011 by Ellen Schwartz
Recipes courtesy of Merri Schwartz

Published in Canada by Tundra Books,
75 Sherbourne Street, Toronto, Ontario M5A 2P9

Published in the United States by Tundra Books of Northern New York,
P.O. Box 1030, Plattsburgh, New York 12901

Library of Congress Control Number: 2010928807

Library and Archives Canada Cataloguing in Publication

Schwartz, Ellen, 1949-
The case of the missing deed / Ellen Schwartz.

(Teaspoon detectives)
For ages 8-11.
ISBN 978-0-88776-959-7

I. Schwartz, Ellen, 1949- . Teaspoon detectives. II. Title.

PS8587.C578C37 2011   jC813.'54   C2010-903182-2

We acknowledge the financial support of the Government of Canada through
the Book Publishing Industry Development Program (BPIDP) and that of the
Government of Ontario through the Ontario Media Development Corporation's
Ontario Book Initiative. We further acknowledge the support of the Canada
Council for the Arts and the Ontario Arts Council for our publishing program.

Design: Leah Springate

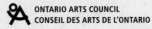

ONTARIO ARTS COUNCIL
CONSEIL DES ARTS DE L'ONTARIO

Printed and bound in Canada

This book was produced using ancient-forest friendly paper.

1 2 3 4 5 6   16 15 14 13 12 11

For Merri – *chef extraordinaire*

In memory of my mother

CONTENTS

"I NEED YOUR HELP"

"Come on, Charlie, pass them!"

Claire, sitting in the backseat between her brother and sister, leaned forward, pointing through the windshield. Up ahead, her cousins' car was winding its way along the coast road, Alex and Olivia waving from the back window. Ever since the two families had driven onto Otter Island from their respective ferries – Claire's from Vancouver and her cousins' from Victoria – and set off for Grandma's cottage, Claire and Alex had been in a race to see who could get there first. Sometimes Aunt Meg's car led, and sometimes, when the road was clear, Charlie pulled ahead, and then Claire gleefully thumbed her nose as they passed.

But now they were behind.

Claire's mom, Eve, turned around and patted her daughter's hand. "Not on this stretch, honey. It's too dangerous."

"But I want to beat them," Claire said, even though she knew her mom was right. Following the south shore of the island, the road curved sharply around coves and bays.

"Let's just get there in one piece," Charlie, her mom's boyfriend, said.

"But we're almost there," Claire said.

"Oh, are we?" her older brother Sébastien said, looking up from his book, *Advanced Sudoku*.

"Gen, time to log off," Eve said to her older daughter.

Geneviève, hunched over her cell phone with fingers flying, didn't respond.

"Geneviève!" Eve said sharply.

She looked up. "Huh?"

"Would you turn your phone off –" Eve began.

"But I'm in the middle of a text to Natalie," she protested. "Oh! They're all at the pool. Aaron too." Her fingers flew.

Turning around, Eve grumbled to Charlie, "I'd like to pitch that thing into the sea."

He reached across the front car seat and squeezed her shoulder. "Never mind, Eve. You were thirteen once."

Eve just grunted.

When they came to the last straight stretch, Claire urged, "Come on, Charlie, go for it!" But before he could do anything, Aunt Meg and Uncle Tony's car turned onto the winding gravel driveway that led up to Grandma's cottage.

"Phooey," Claire said. "Alex'll never let me hear the end of it."

Charlie chuckled and then hit the brakes as Aunt Meg's car suddenly slowed in front of him. A cloud of dust arose.

"What's wrong?" Claire said.

Charlie shrugged, slowing down more as Aunt Meg's car crawled over to the side. Charlie followed. A moment later, Claire saw why. An unfamiliar car was driving down Grandma's driveway. It was silver, sleek, and sporty, with a convertible top rolled up. As it approached, carefully passing Aunt Meg's car and pulling up to theirs, Claire could see three people behind the closed windows: a man driving, a woman beside him, and another man in the back seat.

"Who're they?" Claire asked.

"Don't know," Eve answered. "Not islanders, I'm sure. And why they were at Grandma's I have no idea —"

Just then the car pulled even with Charlie's, and Claire spotted a logo on the side door. Within a circle, there was a blue lake with a purple mountain rising behind it and, beneath the top curve of the circle, two words in bold letters.

"TANTALUS MINING," Claire read aloud. "What's that?"

Sébastien sat forward. "It's that mining company — you remember, the one that wants to put the mine on Lookout Hill."

Sébastien knew about Tantalus Mining. Grandpa had told him about it six months earlier, shortly before he died. Apparently there was a deposit of something called tantalum on the island — and it was a real mineral; he and Grandpa had looked it up on the Internet. Tantalus Mining had announced plans to dig a mine right in the middle of Otter Island. They wanted to buy up all the properties around the mine site, and on the way to it, too. And that included Grandma and Grandpa's.

Before Grandpa got really sick, he and a group of islanders had met to talk about how they could stop the mine. They'd written letters to the *Otter Observer*. Stan Wilensky, the unofficial "mayor" of Otter Island, had replied, saying that there was nothing to worry about, that the mine, when it came, would be good for the island, and that Tantalus would do everything properly, "because they truly care about our beautiful environment."

Sébastien could still remember Grandpa's snort at that one.

Then Grandpa had gotten more and more ill, and the family had stopped worrying about the mine.

Now the silver car eased past Charlie's, followed by a puff of dust. For a moment, the driver looked toward Charlie's car, and Sébastien's eyes locked with his. The man looked angry, Sébastien thought. His hands were clenching the steering wheel, and his mouth was drawn in a line.

"What could they have wanted with Mom?" Eve wondered in a worried voice.

"Maybe it has something to do with the open house tomorrow," Charlie said.

Maybe so, Sébastien thought. Grandma had called and asked them to accompany her to the meeting that Tantalus Mining was holding to present their plans to the islanders. Since the family was intending to come for their annual summer visit anyway, they'd moved up their plans to arrive a couple of days early.

The car moved on. Aunt Meg pulled back onto the driveway, and Charlie followed. Half a minute later, both cars had parked on a gravel pullout beside the cottage, and everyone was piling out. But instead of hugging and kissing and hauling out their gear – the backpacks and coolers, Alex and Claire's fishing rods, Olivia and Aunt Meg's paints and brushes, the groceries and books and beach shoes and beer – everyone rushed inside to see how Grandma was.

She was in the kitchen, leaning on the counter. Her shoulders were shaking.

"Mom!" Eve said, rushing over. "What's the matter?"

Aunt Meg took Grandma's hand. "Who were those people? What did they do to you?"

"Grandma, don't cry," Alex said, patting her on the back.

Grandma wiped her eyes with her free hand. When she turned to face them, Sébastien was shocked. Grandma was so thin, it looked like she'd barely been eating. Her gray hair, normally wavy, was an unkempt mess. Her whole body looked . . . caved in. His mother exchanged an alarmed look with Aunt Meg.

Sure, Sébastien knew that Grandma was sad over Grandpa's death. They all were. The last few times he'd seen Grandma, she'd been down in the dumps. Her voice had sounded flat. She'd stopped painting. When he'd told her about the science prize he'd won, she'd said, "That's nice, dear," as if she hadn't really heard.

But this was worse. Now she looked . . . old . . . tired . . . and very upset.

"I'm going to lose the cottage!" she wailed.

Uncle Tony, a giant at six foot four, put his arm around his mother-in-law. "Here, Lily, sit down." He gently guided her to a chair. Charlie filled a glass with water as the others clustered around.

"Now, tell us everything, Mom," Eve said.

"It's about that mine, isn't it?" Aunt Meg said.

Wiping her eyes, Grandma nodded.

"What did those Tantalus people say to you?"

"Well, you know they've been coming around, trying to get me to sell them my property for the road to the mine."

"But you refused," Claire said.

"Of course she refused!" Alex said. He turned to his grandmother. "There's no way you'd sell this place, right, Grandma?"

"Of course not. And I don't have to sell. They can't make me. If I don't, they'll have to go around me. But today they said . . . they said that whether I sell or not, I've got to prove that I own the property. And if I don't, then the land will go back to the government, who owned it in the first place, and then the government will give it to them for the mine." Her lip trembled.

"But of course you own the place!" Aunt Meg said. "You and Daddy bought it fair and square."

"Meg's right, Lily," Uncle Tony said. "You've got yourself into a state for nothing. You'll show them the deed, and that'll be the end of that."

"But I can't find it! I can't remember where it is!" Grandma burst into tears again.

Eve and Aunt Meg both started patting their mother on the back.

Sniffling, Grandma wiped her eyes. "The crazy thing is, Sam told me where it was, before he died. He was sure something bad was going to happen with the mine and that we'd need to fight for our land. So he sat me down and said, 'Lil, you've got to remember this: the deed is . . . '"

She shook her head. "But he was so sick at the time, and I was so worn-out from taking care of him, and I had a million things on my mind – and it didn't sink in. It just went in one ear and out the other. I've wracked my brain. I've thought and thought. But I can't remember. And I'm so afraid of losing the cottage!" She put her face in her hands.

"I don't understand," Charlie said, sounding puzzled. "Wouldn't the deed be in a safety deposit box in a bank? That's the logical place to keep important papers like that."

Eve, Aunt Meg, and Uncle Tony all exchanged looks.

"Ah, but Sam wasn't logical when it came to that sort of thing," Uncle Tony said. "Didn't like to keep documents in the bank."

"Why not?" Charlie asked.

Eve shrugged. "Who knows? He was a brilliant man, but when it came to things like this, he was . . . odd, shall we say." She smiled fondly.

"He used to say, 'Who knows who's snooping around those boxes?'" Aunt Meg added. "So he hid important papers all over the place."

"Birth certificates in the freezer," Sébastien said.

"Our marriage certificate under a loose floorboard," Grandma added with a sniffle. "An insurance policy inside a broken toaster. Or was it a stereo?"

"I thought it was that old blender," Eve replied, and everybody laughed.

"And then he made up clues to tell you where everything was and hid them in places where he knew you'd find them," Uncle Tony added. "Like, *Brrr!* It was freezing the day you were born, to hint that the birth certificate was in the freezer."

Charlie shook his head. "He sounds like a real eccentric."

"The most wonderful eccentric who ever lived," Grandma said, managing a smile. "But what am I going to do? I can't lose this place. Sam would die if he knew." As if hearing what she'd just said, she burst out laughing, then back into tears again.

Uncle Tony reached over and placed his big hand on Grandma's arm. "Don't worry, Lily. You won't lose it. We'll find the deed. We'll tear the house apart if we have to."

"But I already have!" Grandma said. "I've gone through every room, every drawer, every cupboard. It's not there. It's not anywhere."

"It has to be somewhere," Uncle Tony said. "It can't have disappeared."

"And now you've got us," Alex added. "More eyes and hands. Come on, everybody, let's look!"

"That's the spirit," Aunt Meg said, jumping up. "We'll split up and search. Tony and I'll take the kitchen."

"Charlie and I'll take the living room," Eve said.

"I'll search Grandpa's study," Sébastien offered, starting up the stairs. "And you can help, Alex. Come on."

"I'll do Grandma's studio," Olivia said. "Grandma, you come with me."

"But I've already looked in there."

"But I can climb up on the drafting table and look on top of the cupboards," Olivia said. "Bet you didn't do that, did you?"

Geneviève turned to Claire. "Guess we're doing the bedrooms."

Sighing, Claire followed her sister up the stairs. "How come I never get to pick first? Just because I'm only nine and I'm the baby of the family –"

Eve lightly swatted her on the bottom. "Oh, poor Claire. Bring out the violins."

—●

At first there was an excited hum as everyone scattered throughout the cottage.

In the kitchen, Aunt Meg and Uncle Tony emptied cupboards, clattering baking pans and soup pots and mixing bowls onto the counters, then putting them back. They went through every napkin, placemat, dish towel, and tablecloth. They even took Grandma's entire recipe collection – a grab bag of notebooks, file boxes, cookbooks, and scraps torn from magazines, all scrawled with handwritten scribbles, dotted with sticky notes, and splattered with food stains – from the pantry shelves and rifled through them to see if anything resembling a deed fell out.

Upstairs, Claire looked under Grandma's pillows, felt under her mattress, and got down on the floor to peer under the bed. Straightening up, she saw that her sister was sitting on a chair, hunched over her cell phone.

"Gen?"

No response.

"Gen!"

"What?" Geneviève looked up. A flush spread over her face.

"What're you doing?" Claire asked. "We're supposed to be looking for Grandma's deed."

"I know, but –"

"Don't you care?"

"Of course I do!" Geneviève snapped. And she did, she really did, she thought, shutting her phone with a sigh. It was just that all her friends were back home, swimming, riding bikes, getting ice cream, flirting. And here she was, a ferry ride away and completely out of reach, missing it all.

But still, she had to do her part to help Grandma. And she wanted to. The possibility of Grandma losing the cottage was just too awful to think about. She put down her phone and helped Claire go through the dresser drawers. No sign of a piece of paper.

"Hey, Gen, look at this," Claire said with a giggle, pointing to Grandma's old-fashioned bras and roll-up stockings.

"Sex-y!" Geneviève said with a laugh.

Still giggling, Claire opened another drawer – and froze when she saw that it was empty. Grandpa's drawer. She leaned down and sniffed. It still smelled like him: a mix of his minty aftershave and the old, threadbare shirts he'd refused to get rid of, giving off scents of salt and sea. Claire teared up. Geneviève threw her arms around her sister.

———•

In the study, Alex went to Grandpa's big oak desk and pored through envelopes and stamps, pens and erasers and calculators. "I'm sure we'll find it in here. After all, this is where Grandpa kept all his important stuff, right, Seb?"

"Right," Sébastien said, scanning the room. Where would Grandpa hide such an important paper? His eyes lit on the bookshelf. Of course. Grandpa loved books, all kinds, especially those that he kept in his study: there were math books – Grandpa had been a math teacher on the mainland before he and Grandma retired to Otter Island – books of riddles and word puzzles, and spy books full of mysteries and ciphers. Energetically, Sébastien started taking the books off the shelf, one at a time, shaking them and putting them back. He remembered the fun he and Grandpa had had together, solving complicated math problems, trying to stump each other with riddles, racing to unscramble secret codes.

Book after book. Nothing.

———•

In the studio, Olivia flipped through stacks of canvases and crawled into lower cupboards, peering into their back corners. She even took down the framed paintings hanging on the walls and looked on their back surfaces. "That's where they hide secret messages in the movies, you know, Grandma," she said. But nothing was taped to the back of any of them.

At first Grandma helped, emptying the turpentine cupboard and going through her drawers of oil paints. Olivia climbed up on the drafting table and checked the tops of the cupboards. After a while Grandma sat down, chin in hand. Olivia kept looking.

━━●

Eve and Charlie looked under couch cushions, peered beneath the stereo, and rifled through shelves of records and CDs in the living room. Eve turned to the two easy chairs that sat in front of the big bay window overlooking the sea. She sighed. "I can just see my parents sitting in those chairs. They must've spent years in them."

Charlie put his arm around her. "I don't blame them, with this view." Beyond the deck, with its glider and Adirondack chairs, the lawn sloped down to meet the beach. The dock jutted out into the water, with a small boat shed off to the side. On the horizon, a sailboat scudded by, its sails stiff in the breeze, and the ferry could just be seen rounding the curve, heading toward the east side of the island.

Charlie opened the cupboards beneath the bay window. "What's this?" he asked. Instead of books or keepsakes, which he'd expected to find, the space was filled with what looked like old wooden boards, standing vertically, weathered and gray.

"Oh, that," Eve said with a laugh. "That's the old wall."

"The what?"

She knelt and stroked the weathered wood. "When my parents first came to Otter Island and found this property, the cottage was a wreck. They tore down most of it, but kept this one section of the wall and built around it."

"Why?"

Eve smiled. "Because this was where they fell in love with the place. Dad wanted to keep a little bit of it alive."

Charlie shook his head. "What a character. I wish I'd gotten to know him better."

"So do I."

They stood for a moment, then Charlie shut the cupboard doors.

—•—

Little by little, the chatter stilled. The laughter died out. The frantic motion slowed down.

The family gathered in the living room. No one needed to say anything. Slumped shoulders and downcast eyes told of failure.

"I knew it," Grandma said.

"Now, don't give up, Mom," Aunt Meg said. "We haven't looked in every corner yet."

"We'll try again," Uncle Tony said. "We'll find it, you'll see, Lily."

Grandma just shook her head. "It's no use. It's gone. I'm going to lose the cottage." She started crying again, silently this time, hopelessly, not even bothering to wipe the tears from her cheeks.

She turned and started trudging up the stairs.

TWO

COLORED RED ON THE MAP

O tter Island Community Hall was packed. Rows of folding chairs had been set up, filling the floor. On the low stage at the front there was a microphone stand and three chairs.

As he entered the room beside Grandma, Sébastien felt her flinch. He followed her eyes. She was staring at a large screen on the stage where a laptop projected the mountain-and-lake logo Sébastien had seen on the company's car the day before. The words TANTALUS MINING: MINING A BETTER TOMORROW circled around it.

Sébastien took Grandma's hand. He didn't have to look at her to know that her eyes were bloodshot from lack of sleep. She hadn't wanted to come today. She'd said she just couldn't face hearing about the mine that would soon take away her home. But the rest of the family had insisted. Uncle Tony had reassured her that there was no way she was going to lose her home. Eve had said they'd all be there with her. So Grandma had come.

Sébastien led her across the room to find seats. At once, they were thronged by family friends. Tall, thin Hugh Crombie, Grandpa's best friend, who lived down the road on a cliff the locals called Hugh's Perch, didn't say much; he just gave Grandma's shoulder a squeeze. Muriel, Grandma's good friend, who owned the berry patch and general store, smiled as she hugged Grandma, but Sébastien heard her whisper to his mom, "I'm worried about her, Eve."

Bernie and Leon, Grandpa's old fishing buddies, nodded at Alex and Claire, the two grandchildren who loved fishing the best. "The fish're biting this summer," Leon said. "Won't be the same without Sam . . ." He cleared his throat. "But you two are welcome to join us."

"Thanks, Leon," Claire said.

Leon's wife, Tillie, who ran Tillie's Café near the ferry dock, shrieked when she spied the kids. "My God, how you've grown! You," she said to Sébastien, ruffling his hair, "are turning into a beanpole. And look at this gorgeous young woman," she said to Geneviève.

Geneviève turned pink. It sounded a bit dorky, but still it was cool to be called a young woman. She was, after all, thirteen. Almost grown up.

Twisting so her mom wouldn't see, she turned on her cell phone. A beep told her she had a text message. It was from Natalie. She opened it eagerly, anxious to know what her friends were up to and whether they missed her like she missed them. Most of all, she wanted to find out what was going on with Aaron. Natalie had said she'd keep an eye on him for her. Not that he was *hers,* of course, Geneviève thought. Nothing like that. Still, it was good to know that her best friend was watching out for her.

The text had been sent late the night before: "ME + AARON! HOT FUN IN COOL POOL Y-DAY!"

Geneviève sat there for a moment, stunned. Then she texted back, "HOW COULD U?"

Natalie *knew* she liked Aaron, *knew* she was looking

forward to hanging out with him when she got back. What was she up to?

Of course, there was nothing official going on between Geneviève and Aaron, just a little harmless flirting so far. She'd threatened to spy on him in the guys' change room at the pool. He'd teased her about her performance in the end-of-year school talent show. They'd exchanged a few texts, signed with x's and o's.

Natalie knew all that. And she'd made a move on him anyway.

Oh, if only Geneviève was there! She could flirt with Aaron and get him back.

Or could she?

Geneviève felt tears coming. Quickly, she slipped out of her seat and ran to the bathroom.

—◆—

"Ladies and gentlemen, we're about to begin, so please take your seats," boomed a voice over the microphone. Sébastien helped Grandma to a chair and sat down next to her.

Three people, two men and a woman, stepped onto the stage. One of the men stood at the microphone, while the other two sat down. "Good afternoon, everyone, and thank you for coming out today," said the man. "My name is Mark Saxby, and these are my associates, Valerie London and Wayne Cheng. We're from Tantalus Mining, and we want to welcome you to our open house."

Sébastien recognized Mark Saxby as the man who'd driven the car the day before, and the other two as his passengers. Unlike the islanders, most of whom were in T-shirts and shorts or sundresses, the three company people were all dressed up. The men were in dark suits and crisp white shirts. Mark Saxby had a blue tie with red stripes, and Wayne Cheng had a red tie with blue stripes. Valerie London wore a slim skirt, silky blouse, and high heels, with a gleam of gold at her throat.

Next to him, Sébastien heard Grandma clear her throat nervously. He gave her hand a pat.

———•

Crap! They've started, Geneviève thought as she reentered the hall. As she squeezed down the row toward her seat, her mother shot her a look. Geneviève knew she'd hear about it later, but right now she didn't care. Her heart was broken, and that was all that mattered.

As she turned before taking her seat, she caught sight of an unfamiliar blond head across the room. It was a kid, a guy, about her age. *Strange*, she thought. She knew most of the kids on the island, at least by sight, and she'd never seen this guy before. For a moment he looked up, and their eyes locked. *Wow*, she thought. At this distance, all she could make out was sun-bleached hair, bronzed skin, and dark eyes, but . . . *wow.*

Who was he?

———•

Mark Saxby rested his arm on the microphone stand. "We're here to tell you about our plans and answer any questions you may have," he said. "And this isn't a one-way street. We want to dialogue with you so this becomes a win-win for everyone." He beamed at the crowd.

A loud snort came from Hugh. Several people laughed.

Mark Saxby kept smiling. "Now, to begin, I want to ask *you* a few questions. Is there anyone here who has a cell phone? Raise your hand if you have a cell phone."

There were some puzzled glances. Many people, including Geneviève, raised their hands.

"Good. Now, how about PDAs, or personal digital assistants? Can we have a show of hands if you own one of those?"

Fewer hands went up. Eve's was one of them.

"Thank you. And finally, pagers. Anyone have a pager?"

A dozen or so hands were raised. Murmurs rumbled. "What's this about?" "Who cares?"

Mark Saxby smiled. "Ladies and gentlemen, if you raised your hand, you are one of the millions of people around the world who use tantalum. What's tantalum, you ask? To answer that question, I'll turn the floor over to my colleague, Dr. Wayne Cheng. He's the engineer in the group and handles the scientific issues."

The other man stood up. He didn't look as relaxed as Mark Saxby. The part in his black hair was razor straight. He stood with his palms flat against his sides. He faced the audience and, staring at a point over their heads, recited, "Tantalum is a rare chemical element with the symbol Ta and the atomic number 73. It's a hard, blue-gray, lustrous metal. Tantalum is used in manufacturing cell phones, pagers, and personal computers."

He sat down.

Mark Saxby moved back to center stage. "Thank you, Wayne. So you see, folks, tantalum is vital to our modern communications. And you are very lucky to have a sizable deposit of this rare and valuable mineral right here on Otter Island."

"Quit the sell job and just tell us about the land grab," Bernie said.

Mark Saxby's jaw clenched, but his smile stayed in place. "I wouldn't exactly call it that, sir. We call it our land acquisition program. But I'll be pleased to explain it."

He clicked a computer mouse, and a map of Otter Island filled the screen. The town center with the float-plane dock, Emergency Station and lighthouse, ferry dock, general store, café, and picnic area were all marked on the northeast side of the island. The public beach was labeled on the southeast shore. Lookout Hill, a large area in the middle of the island, was colored green, with the words MINE SITE written on it. A spiral inside the green area indicated Lookout Hill Road. Other areas, on the south and west parts of the island, were colored red, and a thick dotted line, marked ACCESS ROAD, wound through the red areas to the mine site. Within the green and red areas were dotted several small yellow squares.

"That's my home," Grandma said in a strangled voice, pointing to a beachfront rectangle covered in red.

Grandma's property wasn't the only red one, Sébastien saw. So were Hugh's Perch, Muriel's berry patch, Bernie's place, Leon and Tillie's land, and dozens more properties.

Mark Saxby pointed to one of the yellow squares. "These represent the properties we've purchased so far. As you can see, many Otter Island residents have already come aboard. The properties within the red and green zones, that aren't yellow yet, are still in negotiation."

"We'll never sell!" Tillie yelled.

"You tell 'im, Tillie," Muriel said, knitting needles clacking.

Mark Saxby nodded. "That is your choice – as long as you hold clear title to your property, of course. If not, the land will revert to the government, and they will decide what to do with it. We believe they will turn over those properties to us for the benefit of the project, but that is up to them."

Grandma made a distressed sound. Sébastien patted her hand.

"Now, if you choose to sell, you'll be given fair market value for your property. If not, we will be forced to build around you. Naturally, we hope everyone will join us. But it's up to each of you. After all," he said, spreading his hands, "it's a free country."

"Yeah, you're free to get rich by wrecking our island," said Kevin, a member of the Saanich band who ran the Emergency Station next to the lighthouse.

Mark Saxby ignored the comment. "As you may know," he said, "we have applied to the government for a permit to operate the mine. In order to receive the permit, we have to meet three requirements. First, we have to submit an economic report showing how the mine will benefit the island's economy. Second, we have to do an environmental assessment showing that the mine will have little or no impact on the environment. And third, we have to do public consultation. I'm happy to tell you that Tantalus is meeting all three of these requirements. So first, to tell you about the economic report, I'd like to call on Valerie."

The woman stood up, smoothing her skirt and smiling. "Thank you, Wayne," she said, "and good afternoon, everyone." When you see how great the mine will be for Otter Island's economy, I'm sure you will be as excited about it as we are."

There were several snorts. But there were also some murmurs of "Yes" and "Let's hear it" from the side of room where Stan Wilensky was seated.

The cover page of an official-looking report filled the screen. OTTER ISLAND TANTALUM MINE: ECONOMIC REPORT, it read. London clicked the mouse, and a graph appeared. "This shows that 72.6 full-time jobs will be created by the mine," she said.

"I feel sorry for the point-six guy," someone said, and some people snickered.

London went to the next page. This was a chart full of numbers and dollar signs. Down the left column, all the businesses and shops on the island were listed: Tillie's Café, Wilensky Air, Beachside Bed and Breakfast, and so on. As the columns moved to the right, the numbers got bigger and bigger.

"As you can see, virtually every business on the island stands to get more business as a result of workers flooding in. And then, when they finish their jobs and tell their friends how terrific Otter Island is, tourism here will go through the roof!"

"Too bad there'll be nothing left to see," Bernie called out.

"Don't worry, Bernie, they can go for a tour of the beautiful mine," Leon said.

London continued clicking through the pages, going over all the great things Otter Island would get from the mine. New roads. Better float-plane service. A real estate boom, as construction workers and others bought homes here. Money from the sale of the tantalum.

The screen returned to the Tantalus Mining logo.

"You can pick up a copy of the economic report and read

all the exciting details," London said. "But take it from me, with this mine, Otter Island has hit the economic jackpot!"

There was a smattering of handclapping from the side of the room. Sébastien turned. Stan Wilensky, of course, was clapping. Next to him, also clapping, was Ted Crombie, Hugh's son. *That's odd,* Sébastien thought, *since Hugh is so opposed to the mine.* He looked at Hugh. A flush had spread up his face, and he was frowning.

Mark Saxby strolled back to center stage. "Thank you, Valerie. Now, ladies and gentlemen, we'd like to present our environmental report. Here again is our resident scientist, Dr. Wayne Cheng. Wayne."

Cheng stood up, straightening his tie. He cleared his throat. "Yes," he said, "we – that is, I – found that the tantalum mine will have little or no environmental impact on Otter Island."

"What!" several people shouted at once.

As Cheng clicked the computer mouse and turned toward the screen, Sébastien noticed that he wasn't just stiff. He seemed uneasy, as if he didn't want to be up there. Maybe he just didn't like speaking in public. *Can't blame him,* Sébastien thought. He didn't much like it himself. Still, Cheng seemed awfully uncomfortable.

The lights went down, and the title of another report appeared: OTTER ISLAND TANTALUM MINE: ENVIRONMENTAL REPORT, by Dr. Wayne Cheng.

He clicked the mouse, and the title "Waste Management Solved" appeared. Beneath it, a mathematical equation said:

WASTE ROCK = STORED ROCK = ZERO WASTE PROBLEM

"Now, it is true that the mining operations will produce a great deal of waste rock," Cheng said. "All mining does. But this will not be a problem because we will store the rock in a temporary, sustainable, state-of-the-art containment system during the mining phase, and then bury it all back inside the mine once the tantalum has been removed."

"How is a huge, ugly rock pile a 'sustainable' whosit whatsit containment system?" Muriel asked, but Cheng had moved on to the next slide. It showed a chunk of silver-blue rock, light glinting off its cut surfaces.

"You will no doubt be relieved to know that tantalum is inert –"

"What's that mean?" someone called out.

"It means that it doesn't break down easily," Cheng explained. "So there will be no toxic emissions into the land, air, or water."

Click. A page titled "Impacts on Fish and Wildlife" came up. "No bird colonies or salmon stocks will be endangered by our operations," Cheng said. "And if they are, we have solutions. We'll relocate the birds to other nesting trees. We'll stock other streams with salmon fry. Everything will balance out."

"That's ridiculous!" yelled Chad, a young man who'd recently moved to the island and was an avid birdwatcher.

"You can't just move birds' nests – they'll never survive!" said his wife, Rachel.

"And dumping salmon fry into other streams doesn't work," Leon shouted. "They'll die!"

Cheng didn't respond. Wiping his brow, he clicked the mouse. A list of phrases appeared: Appropriate waste management. Fish and wildlife protected. No effects on land, air, or water. Next to each one was a big red check mark.

"To conclude, our study found that, for all these reasons, the tantalum mine is an environmentally sound project and can go ahead."

Quickly, Dr. Wayne Cheng sat down.

The room filled with shouts.

"What about the noise and pollution from the trucks?"

"And the dust?"

"And the traffic? I'd call those environmental impacts. You didn't talk about any of them!"

"No effect on birds? Where's the proof?" Rachel said.

Chad nodded. "Yeah, let's see that environmental report."

Mark Saxby strolled back to center stage. "That report is being printed as we speak," he said smoothly, "so unfortunately, we don't have copies on hand today. But if you pop into the office in a few days, we'll be glad to give you one. Besides, not wasting paper is part of Tantalus Mining's commitment to being environmentally responsible."

There were loud guffaws at that.

"Now, ladies and gentlemen, we've presented our economic and environmental reports. That leaves only the third requirement, to hold public consultation. And that's what we've just finished doing. As soon as we can write up a report on today's open house, we will submit all three reports to the government, and we will have met all the requirements for the permit."

"You call this a public consultation?" Hugh shouted. "It's a whitewash!"

"Yeah, you didn't consult. You just told us what you were going to do!" Kevin added.

Saxby went on as if no one had spoken. "We expect to receive the permit shortly, in a week or ten days. Once the permit is issued, you must decide immediately whether to sell or not. And I can tell you that the prices we will be offering then will not be as high as they are right now. So sell now and get all the value you can out of your property!"

The meeting ended. Chairs scraped, and the swell of conversation filled the room. Neighbors gathered in small groups, debating the pros and cons of the mine, of selling or holding on to their properties, of the future of Otter Island.

Grandma stood up, clutching the back of a chair. "Take me home," she said.

At the word *home,* her voice broke. Eve took one arm, Aunt Meg the other, and surrounded by the rest of the family, they headed out of the hall.

THREE

A PASSION FOR PESTO

Alex was awakened the next morning by the soft brush of a kiss on his cheek. He opened sleepy eyes to see his mom and dad and remembered they were going home to Victoria, to work, and would be back in a week to pick him and Olivia up. He said good-bye and rolled over to go back to sleep. Beside him, in a sleeping bag on the floor, Sébastien snored softly.

Alex closed his eyes, but he didn't feel sleepy anymore. He tried to slide back into the dream he'd been having, about kicking the winning soccer goal, but it refused to let him in. He thought about how cozy he was in the sleeping bag and took slow, deep breaths. Nothing worked. He couldn't get back to sleep, and he knew why.

Grandma.

She looked terrible. She wasn't eating. She probably wasn't sleeping. She was nervous and upset and sad – not like the old Grandma he knew and loved.

Something had to be done. But what? They'd searched the cottage for the deed, and even though it had to be there some-where, they were all stumped. Without it, Grandma would lose the cottage, and that would be –

No. It was too horrible to think about.

Again, his mind came back to the thought: *We've got to do something. I've got to do something.*

But what?

No clue.

Oh, if only Grandpa were here, Alex thought, rolling onto his back and gazing at the ceiling. If he were, Alex would get him to go fishing, and while they were drifting in the canoe, the only sound the plop of their lines hitting the water, he'd say, "Grandpa, Grandma's in trouble. What can we do?"

And Grandpa would say . . .

But that's the trouble, Alex thought, flopping over again. *Grandpa isn't here, and there are no answers, and everything is a muddle.*

Wide awake now, he slid out of his sleeping bag – careful not to wake Sébastien – put on his glasses, got dressed, and tiptoed downstairs. Passing the living room, he saw that the girls were still asleep, Geneviève on the couch and Claire and Olivia on the floor.

Entering the kitchen, Alex spotted a box on the counter. *Heaven Preserve Us* it said. *Yum!* That was Muriel's company. With the berries she harvested from her patch, she made jams, preserves, syrups – and delicious muffins. He opened the box. Twelve plump blueberry muffins sat in rows.

For a moment, Alex stood there, puzzled. How had they got there? Had his parents gone to Muriel's general store at the crack of dawn, driven back to the cottage, and then left again for the ferry? No, that didn't make sense. But then . . . ?

A peal of laughter coming from the beach gave him the answer. He looked out the window. Yup – Aunt Eve and Charlie. They were strolling, hand in hand, near the water's edge. He couldn't hear what they were saying, but their laughter carried on the breeze.

Alex knew that Sébastien didn't like his mom's new boy-friend, but Alex thought Charlie was okay. Although if *his* parents split up and *his* mom showed up with a new guy, Alex knew he wouldn't like it one bit either. So he couldn't blame his cousin.

Alex took a muffin and bit in. Mmm . . . The blueberries were juicy and sweet. Muriel sure was a good cook.

Of course, Alex thought loyally, she wasn't the only one. Grandma was too. Or at least she used to be. Alex sighed, remembering how they'd all wander into the kitchen on summer mornings, sleepy and hungry, to find Grandma making fruit salad and omelets and cinnamon rolls, her cheeks flushed and her apron spotted with berry juice.

Suddenly he had an idea.

—•

One by one the cousins straggled into the kitchen: first Claire, wide awake and instantly ready to go out and play; then Sébastien, his dirty blond hair hanging in his eyes, a book of Grandpa's brainteasers tucked under his arm; next Olivia, her glasses smudged with charcoal fingerprints, her ever-present sketchbook in hand and a pencil tucked behind her ear; and finally Geneviève, her eyes bloodshot as if she hadn't slept well, already flipping open her phone.

Alex waited until each of them had discovered the box and chomped down on a muffin. Then he told them about his idea for cheering Grandma up.

—•

The five of them stood outside Grandma's door, hesitating. Alex knocked softly. There was no answer. He opened the door a crack. Grandma was lying in bed, propped up on pillows, gazing out the window. In her hand was a crumpled tissue.

"Grandma?" he said. "Can we come in?"

"Sure," she said in a flat voice.

They arranged themselves around her.

"Grandma . . ." Alex began, "would you come down and cook for us?"

"Cook what, honey?"

"Anything."

"How about your fresh pea soup?" Olivia said.

"Or peach cobbler?" said Sébastien.

"With ice cream," Claire added. "Yum!"

The others giggled, but Grandma just lay there. Alex shot Geneviève a look. Strange that she wasn't chiming in, suggesting dishes. After all, she was the one who loved to cook with Grandma. *She looks kind of distracted,* he thought.

"We miss you, Grandma," Olivia said.

"And we know how you love cooking, so we thought –" Alex stopped. Then he plunged on. "We thought it would cheer you up."

Tears filled Grandma's eyes, and she choked back a sob. "I'm sorry, but . . . I just don't feel up to it."

"But Grandma, it'll make you feel better," Claire said.

"I'm afraid not, sweetheart."

Alex knew there was no point pushing her. He stood, and the others followed his lead. "Okay, Grandma, it was just a thought. We'll leave you alone."

Silently they went downstairs and sat around the kitchen table.

"Now what?" Olivia said.

"I don't know," replied Alex. "All I know is that I can't stand seeing Grandma like that."

Olivia opened her sketchbook and started drawing a picture of Grandma in the kitchen, whipping up something in a big bowl. Sébastien looked over her shoulder. She'd made only a few marks on the page, a thick line here, a squiggle there, but somehow they conveyed the energy and hubbub of Grandma cooking. Amazing.

"Maybe," he said, thinking aloud, watching Olivia's pencil fly, "if we can't get her to cook, we can cook *for* her."

Alex looked at him. "You mean . . . try and get her to eat?"

"Yeah, fatten her up. She's so skinny."

"Good idea, Seb," Claire said.

"What do you think, Gen?"

Everyone turned to Geneviève, who was staring off into space.

"Gen!" Sébastien said sharply. "We're talking about what we can do for Grandma. Do you care?"

"Of course I care," Geneviève shot back. Her cheeks colored. "I just . . . have other things on my mind at the moment."

"Well, stop thinking about yourself and start thinking about Grandma –"

"Don't you tell me –"

"Guys!" Alex said. "No fighting. Not now." He turned to his cousin. "You're the cook, Gen. What should we make for her?"

Geneviève shrugged. "Let's look in her recipes."

Everyone followed her to the pantry, where Grandma kept her recipe collection. Geneviève started handing them out — the shoebox full of index cards, the manila envelope crammed with slips of paper and magazine clippings, the scribbled-on envelopes held together by an elastic band, the bulging loose-leaf binder, the spiral-bound notebook. They carried them all to the table.

They each grabbed a box or notebook. Sébastien took the loose-leaf binder. It nearly came apart in his hands. The cover, a pebbly black kind of paper, was rubbed thin and torn in places, the cardboard lining poking through. So many extra pages and sticky notes had been added that the notebook gaped wide like an open accordion. It even had a smell, the aroma of ingredients that had splashed or splattered on its pages: vinegar and cinnamon, garlic and chocolate.

He started paging though. In places Grandma had written notes to herself, things like "double the sugar" or "decrease baking time" or "subst. honey for sugar."

"So what does Grandma love?" he asked.

"*Herbed Roasted Chicken,*" Alex said, pointing to a recipe.

"*Lasagna,*" Olivia piped in.

"*Salmon à l'orange,*" said Geneviève. "Remember how good that was?"

"*Chocolate Cake . . . Lightning Cake . . . Angel Food Cake . . . Lemon Pound Cake . . .*" Claire said.

"I asked what Grandma would like, not what you would like," Sébastien teased.

"Grandma loves everything," Geneviève said. "Or at least she used to, before . . ."

"Okay, then what would really grab her? There must be something."

Olivia pulled a recipe out of the shoebox. "*Pesto!*"

"Right, Liv!" Geneviève said. "That's her favorite food in the world. She puts it on everything – pasta, rice, potatoes, sandwiches . . ."

Sébastien chuckled. "One time I caught her putting it on toast – for breakfast!"

"*Pesto* it is, then," Olivia said.

Grandma's Famous Pesto

Ingredients:
1 1/2 cups fresh basil leaves
1 cup fresh parsley
1 tablespoon fresh oregano
1 tablespoon fresh thyme
1 tablespoon fresh rosemary
1 tablespoon fresh tarragon
1/4 cup walnuts
1 or 2 garlic cloves, crushed
1/2 cup grated Parmesan cheese
1/4 cup olive oil
pinch of salt and pepper

Instructions:
1. Preheat oven to 350°.
2. Spread walnuts on a baking sheet and toast in oven until just golden. Cool slightly before using.
3. Pick herbs. *The keystone is the key.*
4. Blend all ingredients in a food processor (or crush using a mortar and pestle) until a smooth paste forms.

5. Refrigerate for up to 1 month (as if it will last that long!).

The cousins checked to see what ingredients were on hand, and Geneviève made a list for the general store.

"What do you suppose this means?" Sébastien said, pointing at the recipe card.

"What?" Olivia peered over his shoulder. "*The keystone is the key*," she read aloud, then shrugged. "No idea. Some kind of note from Grandma to herself about how to prepare the herbs?"

"Isn't that Grandpa's writing?" Sébastien asked.

"Looks like it. I wonder why Grandpa would write on Grandma's recipe," Claire said. "He never cooked."

"Who knows?" Sébastien said. "You know Grandpa – maybe it was a secret love note. Remember that time he hid Grandma's anniversary present in the herb garden and then left her a clue in the bathroom saying '*I'll love you till the end of thyme*'?"

They smiled at the memory.

Just then the door opened. Sébastien turned. It was his mom and Charlie. They laughed as they hopped, first on one foot and then the other, brushing the sand off their feet. They were flushed and windblown.

"Hey, Mom, guess what," Claire said, and started telling them about the plan to cook for Grandma.

"Great idea!" Charlie exclaimed.

Sébastien frowned. It wasn't *his* family, wasn't *his* place to say what was or wasn't good for Grandma. This was *their* cottage, *their* family home.

If only Charlie would just go away.

It wasn't like Sébastien wanted his dad to come back. He knew his parents had been unhappy together. He'd overheard the tense conversations at night when he was in bed. He'd seen the way they avoided each other, his mom always working late at her job in a downtown office, his dad always going out to run errands.

Still, it was a shock when they sat the three children down and announced that they were separating. Sébastien could still remember the feeling of disbelief, the conviction that they couldn't really mean it.

But they did. Soon after, their dad had moved back to Québec. A year or so later he had married again. That was when Sébastien had to admit that his father wasn't coming back.

Which was bad enough.

But then Charlie came onto the scene.

He was a physiotherapist. Eve had gone to see him because of a sore hamstring from running. Next thing Sébastien knew, Charlie was coming over for the odd dinner . . . and then lunch . . . and then staying over on weekends . . . taking his mom out all the time, charming Geneviève and Claire, who couldn't – or wouldn't – see what was going on. And now, here he was, acting like everything was his business. As if he belonged.

Eve gave them money to buy the groceries. "I just hope it works."

"Grandma won't be able to resist our cooking," Alex said.

"Either that, or she won't be able to *digest* your cooking," Charlie teased.

Everyone laughed – except Sébastien. Then they all ran outside for their bikes.

FOUR

LOVE IN THE GROCERY AISLE

Olivia loved Muriel's general store. Being in it was like being inside a kaleidoscope. Whichever way you turned, you got a different view.

On a counter near the entrance, there was an array of Muriel's *Heaven Preserve Us* jams and jellies, sparkling in jewel tones of ruby, purple, and blue. At the back there was a fresh seafood counter, with silver-skinned salmon and trout, blue-black mussels and pearly clams. Along one wall were bins of island produce: lettuce and spinach and chard, bunches of carrots with the dirt still on, plum-sized new potatoes, piles of pea pods. In the middle were shelves of coffee and ketchup, crackers and baby food, spaghetti and pickles. At Muriel's store you could buy Band-Aids and postage stamps and pruning shears and a guide to the best surfing beaches on the island. Just being there made Olivia want to set up an easel and capture it all in dabs of paint.

When the cousins entered, Muriel was in her usual place, perched on a stool at the cash register. Her gray hair, still showing traces of brown, curled around her face.

She was knitting as usual. The scarf she was working on today was green, orange, and pink. Muriel's scarves made of hairy, fluffy yarn reminded Olivia of small porcupines, except that they were in crazy colors: brown and red, purple and orange, yellow and blue and green. In Olivia's opinion, they were hideous, but they flew off the shelves. Evidently there were a lot of color-blind tourists with cold necks.

Muriel waved when they came in. "Hi, kids. How's your grandma today?"

"Not so good," Alex said.

Muriel's brow furrowed. "I've been trying to get her to come over for tea, but she won't." She brightened. "She'll be better now that you're all here."

I hope so, Olivia thought.

"Oh!" Muriel said abruptly. "I just remembered. Guess seeing you all reminded me. Your grandpa gave me a package just before he . . . before. He said it could help your grandma if she needed it. I'll pop over one day and give it to you."

Before Olivia could ask what was in the package, the bell attached to the door tinkled, and Stan Wilensky came in. Olivia knew that Grandma and Grandpa didn't like him. He was always puffed up, acting like he ran Otter Island. And now his picture was plastered all over the place on posters that read, MINING A BETTER TOMORROW FOR OTTER ISLAND!

"Good morning, Muriel," he said with a smile. "I need a few things. I'm treating my staff to a picnic."

"Very nice," Muriel said curtly.

Wilensky went down one of the aisles. As Muriel's knitting needles clacked, the children told her about how Grandma couldn't remember where the deed was hidden, and how they'd searched for it in vain.

"That's awful!" Muriel said. "Without the deed, Lily could lose the place!"

Sébastien nodded. "She's so down, she hardly gets out of bed."

Muriel shook her head.

Walking back toward the cash register, Stan Wilensky pulled out a cell phone. "Forgot what I was supposed to get," he said, chuckling, and dialed a number.

"But that's why we're here," Alex told Muriel. "We're going to cook for her and cheer her up."

"Excellent idea," Muriel said. "Put a few pounds back on those skinny bones. What are you going to make her?"

"Pesto," Olivia said.

Muriel nodded approvingly. "If anything'll bring back Lily's appetite, that will."

The cousins split up to find the ingredients. As Geneviève squatted to lift a bag of walnuts from a low shelf, she heard the doorbell tinkle. A moment later someone walked down her aisle and stopped, scanning the shelves.

Geneviève straightened up and glanced at the person.

It was the guy from the open house. And he was even hotter up close than he was across the room.

She examined him out of the corner of her eye. As she'd thought, he was about her age, maybe a little older, with sun-bleached hair waving down his neck, brown eyes, a small gold earring, skater shorts and worn-out T, and a woven friendship bracelet.

He reached up to the top shelf for a jar of peanut butter. Geneviève put the walnuts in her basket.

He smiled – two dimples, one big and one small, gorgeously lopsided. "Hey."

"Hey."

She stood there stupidly. *Move*, she told herself.

He leaned an arm on the shelf. "You live here?"

"Uh . . . no, just visiting. My grandma. I come every summer." *Shut up!*

"I'm just visiting too. Surfing."

A golden surfer god. *Whoa.*

"I'm Shane."

"Geneviève."

"Cool. So, where do you stay?"

Before she knew it, Geneviève had told him about her grandma, Lily Honeyman, and the cottage and the mine and the missing deed and how she and her sister and brother and cousins were going to try to cheer up their grandmother.

Shane's brown eyes glowed with warmth. "It's awesome that you're doing that for her."

By this time, the others had come to see what was taking Geneviève so long.

"Gen," Sébastien said under his breath, "that's private."

Geneviève flicked her hair over her shoulder. "Ignore my annoying little brother."

Shane smiled. "No worries."

He and Geneviève exchanged cell phone numbers. "See you 'round." With a flash of dimples, he was gone.

Geneviève floated out of the general store.

—●—

"All right, everybody, listen up," Geneviève said, scanning the recipe. They were back in the kitchen. "Alex, you can measure the nuts. Liv, you pick the herbs. Sébastien, you can measure the oil. No, wait, you'll spill it. I'll do it. You can —"

"Whoa!" Sébastien said. "Who died and made you boss?"

"Well, I *am* the most experienced cook. *And* the oldest."

"I thought you had other things on your mind," Sébastien said.

Geneviève blushed. "That's over. And since I'm the only one who knows what they're doing –"

"We're not idiots, you know," Sébastien returned angrily. "The rest of us are actually quite smart."

"Don't worry, Seb, we all know about your genius IQ. You don't have to remind us," Geneviève snapped.

"That's not what I meant!" Even though he was in a gifted program at school, he tried to play it down. And he never claimed to be a genius, for goodness sake.

"All right then, Mister Smarty-pants, you be the chef," Geneviève said.

Sébastien frowned. He didn't know the first thing about cooking – and Geneviève knew it. "Never mind," he mumbled.

Geneviève gave him a smug smile.

"Come on," Olivia said to Sébastien in a low voice. She fetched a basket and a pair of scissors. "Help me with the herbs."

Gratefully, he followed her outside. Anything to get away from his impossible older sister.

Beside the deck there was a patio, tiled in flagstones arranged in a circular pattern: brown, gray, and rust, with one rosy hued slab at the center. On top of the stones were a dozen different herbs in clay pots.

By now it was late morning, and the sun-warmed plants were giving off a delicious fragrance of bark and spice and licorice. Sébastien didn't know one herb from another, but fortunately, Olivia did. He read out the ingredients list – basil, parsley, oregano, thyme, rosemary, and tarragon – and she snipped leaves and stems and put them in the basket.

By the time they came back inside, the nutty smell of roasted walnuts and the aroma of garlic filled the kitchen. The cousins put their ingredients in the blender while Geneviève slowly drizzled in the olive oil. When the pesto was a brilliant green mass, she scraped it into a bowl.

Alex dipped his finger into it and pronounced it delicious.

They cooked a pot of spaghetti and arranged a plate for Grandma on a tray, heaping mounds of pesto on top of the spaghetti and sprinkling extra Parmesan cheese on top. Geneviève folded a cloth napkin in a triangle shape, like she'd seen in a restaurant once. Olivia put a sprig of violets in a small vase.

Grandma was still in bed.

"Surprise, Grandma!" Claire said.

"Look what we made – your favorite!" Alex said.

Grandma's eyes filled with tears. "Oh, how sweet of you."

"Sit up, Grandma, and we'll put the tray on your lap," Olivia said.

She shook her head. "I appreciate it, really I do, but I'm just not hungry. You eat it for me."

"But Grandma, we made this 'specially for you, 'cause we know you love pesto," Claire said. "And there's tons – more than enough for us."

A tear spilled down Grandma's cheek. "I do, and it's such a lovely idea. But I'm just not hungry."

"Just a little bit?" Alex said.

Grandma shook her head. She sighed and turned toward the window.

The cousins looked at one another. Silently they trooped downstairs with the tray.

FIVE

AN EGG-CITING BREAKFAST

The next morning, all five cousins gathered in the kitchen.

"So what should we make for Grandma today?" Geneviève asked. She was smiling, texting on her cell phone.

Claire looked at her in surprise. "What do you mean? We bombed yesterday."

"So what? Maybe we didn't choose the right recipe," Geneviève replied cheerfully. "That doesn't mean we should give up."

"You're in a good mood today," Sébastien said suspiciously.

Geneviève grinned. "Is there a law against that?"

"No, but —"

"I agree with Gen," Alex said. "Grandma's got to eat. We just need to come up with the right dish."

"Which is . . . ?" Sébastien said.

"Well, it's morning," said Geneviève, hitting the Send button and closing her phone. She smiled. "And a beautiful morning at that. What does Grandma like for breakfast?"

Olivia opened her sketchbook and started drawing a breakfast table with a vase of flowers and a steaming cup of coffee. Suddenly her pencil stopped. "*Painterman Eggs.*"

"What's that?" Sébastien said.

"You know, when you make a sunny-side up egg and dip your toast into the yolk, like it's a paintbrush. It's my favorite."

"I never knew those eggs had a name," Claire said. "I just call them sunny-side up eggs."

Olivia shrugged. "Maybe it's just a thing with Grandma and me. I remember when I was little she made them for me one time, and I stuck the end of my toast into the yolk and it went all runny and golden, and I started dabbing it all over my plate, making designs, and Grandma said, 'My little artist. We'll call these *Painterman Eggs* in your honor.'"

"Does she like them?" Alex asked.

"Loves 'em," Olivia said. She paused. "Or at least she used to."

They found the recipe in the manila folder.

Painterman Eggs
Are you feeling artistic this morning?

Ingredients:
(per serving)
1 slice of your favorite bread
1 egg
butter
salt and pepper

Instructions:
1. Melt butter in a small frying pan. When it sizzles, carefully crack an egg into the pan. Cover and cook for a couple of minutes, just until the yolk and white are set. Season with salt and pepper.
2. Meanwhile, toast and butter bread. Cut each slice of toast into long strips.

3. Serve 1 egg and several "paintbrushes" of toast on each plate.
4. With a corner of the toast, pierce the yolk. Use the toast as a paintbrush to dip into the yolk.
5. Don't forget to eat up your "brush" and "paint"!

"There's another one of those funny little notes," Sébastien said, pointing to the phrase beneath the title.

"Looks like Grandpa's writing again, like on the *Pesto* recipe," Olivia said.

"Wonder what he means," said Sébastien.

"Just making a little joke about Grandma being artistic, I guess," Claire said.

Sébastien shook his head. "It's more than a joke. I think it means something."

Geneviève tore herself away from her phone and peered at the note. She flashed a sarcastic smile at her brother. "What, a secret message in the *Painterman Eggs* recipe?" She started wiggling her fingers and making high-pitched, the-aliens-are-coming noises.

Claire giggled.

"Shut up, Gen," Sébastien said.

"Guys," Alex said. He opened the fridge. "We've got bread but no eggs."

A smile spread across Geneviève's face. "What a shame. Guess we've got to go back to the general store."

As they coasted their bikes to a stop in front of the store, Alex pointed across the street. "Isn't that the Tantalus lady?"

Sure enough, outside the offices of the *Otter Observer,* Ted Crombie, the reporter, was talking to Valerie London. She was showing him colorful booklets, and he was taking notes.

"Guess she's giving Ted information about the mine," Gen said.

"Poor Hugh," Alex said.

No one had to ask what he meant. Hugh, their grandfather's best friend, must be heartbroken to think that his son was writing news stories in favor of the mine.

They parked their bikes in the stand in front of the general store. Just then, Shane strolled down the sidewalk.

He came, Geneviève thought, her cheeks growing warm. Who cared about Natalie and Aaron now? Shane was way hotter than Aaron. And he was older. Not a dumb thirteen-year-old. Let Natalie chew on that one.

"Look, it's that kid – what's his name again?" Claire asked.

"Shane," Geneviève whispered. "Sh!"

"What's he doing here?" Sébastien said.

"Hey," Shane said, grinning at Geneviève.

"Hey." The blond streaks in his hair glowed in the sunlight.

"Did you tell him –" Sébastien began. "So *that's* what all the texting was about."

"Shut up, Seb," Geneviève said under her breath.

"Sébastien, isn't it?" Shane said, turning a smile on him.

Ignoring him, Sébastien pushed open the door. The bell tinkled as the others followed him inside.

"Hi, kids!" Muriel said from the cash register, putting down her knitting. The scarf she was working on today was turquoise, mustard yellow, and crimson. "What are you doing back so soon?"

"We're making Grandma *Painterman Eggs* today," Olivia announced.

"How'd the pesto go over?" Muriel asked.

"Not so good. Grandma still isn't eating," Alex told her.

Muriel sighed. "We've got to snap her out of it. But you kids are on the right track. Lily loves food, and sooner or later she'll come around. What do you need?"

"Just eggs," Olivia said.

"And maybe some candy, as long as we're here," Claire added.

"Claire!" Alex said, laughing.

Geneviève and Shane went to get the eggs, while Claire and Alex checked out the candy counter. Olivia perched on a wooden box and started drawing a bunch of beets with their round bulbs and oval-shaped leaves. Sébastien wandered idly up and down the aisles.

The doorbell tinkled. Sébastien heard some people exchange greetings with Muriel. He peeked. It was Rachel and Chad.

"How's it going, you guys?" Muriel said.

Chad sighed. "Not so good, Muriel. We can't get anywhere with our business idea."

"Oh?" Muriel said in that tone that islanders used when they didn't want to pry but were dying with curiosity.

Sébastien was curious too. Rachel and Chad had been living full-time on the island for less than a year. Before that they'd commuted back and forth from their jobs on the mainland. All Sébastien knew about them was that they were into birds. One time when he and Grandpa had run in to them on a hike, they'd gotten into a discussion with Grandpa that lasted half an hour about Pileated Woodpeckers. So what was this about a business? Did it have something to do with the mine?

He sidled closer.

"Well, you know we want to start a business offering bird-watching tours, right?" Rachel said.

Muriel nodded. "Sounds like a great fit for the island."

"But there's so much red tape, we don't know if we'll ever get the permit!"

"And if we don't find some way to make a living here, we're going to have to move back," Chad added in a grim voice.

"We need money," Rachel said. "It's tempting to think of selling our property to Tantalus."

"You wouldn't!" Muriel said.

"No," Chad assured her. "Only as a last resort. But the money sure would come in handy."

Rachel leaned closer to the cash register. "Our neighbors – you know the Wongs, Janet and Ray? – they're thinking about selling. They figure it'll be so awful to have the mining road go around their place, they might as well sell and get something out of it."

Sébastien felt a chill. As one property owner after another sold out, that made it worse for Grandma.

Muriel's knitting needles clacked furiously. "Divide and conquer. That's what they're trying to do," she said, jerking a twisted strand of blue, yellow, and red yarn from her knitting bag.

The cousins came back to the counter with their purchases – Alex had talked Claire into getting only two candy bars – and they paid.

"Good luck," Muriel called after them as they left.

They retrieved their bikes. As Sébastien started pedaling toward home, he saw that Shane and Geneviève were riding double on her bike. Sébastien wheeled around.

"What's going on, Gen?" he said.

"I'm coming too. I want to help," Shane said.

"Isn't that awesome?" Geneviève said, her cheeks pink.

"Gen!" Sébastien rode alongside his sister. "You can't just –"

"Shut *up*, Seb," she hissed.

"Hey, if you don't want me there –" Shane began.

"Ignore him," Geneviève said, giving her brother a dirty look. If Sébastien ruined things with Shane, she'd . . . she'd strangle him. The bike went over a bump, and she rose into the air, landing hard on Shane's lap. "Oops!" she said with a giggle. Shane laughed too.

Furious, Sébastien rode ahead. When he told the others what was happening, they didn't look too happy either, but no one offered to ride back and tell Shane he couldn't come. They were stuck with him.

Geneviève got Sébastien, Claire, Alex, and Olivia to make the toast, while she and Shane fried the eggs. From the other end of the kitchen, Sébastien heard giggling and whispering and saw their two heads, one brown and the other blond, bent together over the stove. Angrily, he cut the toast into strips, slamming his knife into the cutting board. For Grandma's sake, he'd keep his mouth shut.

Geneviève slid a couple of glistening eggs onto a plate and arranged the toast around them in a circle. Olivia made Grandma a cup of tea, with one spoonful of sugar and a drop of milk, just the way she liked it. Alex picked a daisy and placed it on the napkin.

They all stood and regarded the tray.

"Beautiful," Shane said. "She'll love it."

As if you'd know, thought Sébastien.

They took the tray upstairs and knocked on Grandma's door. She was still in bed, and her face looked even paler than before.

"Grandma," Geneviève said brightly, "this is my friend, Shane."

Shane came around the side of the bed and shook Grandma's hand. "I sure hope you'll feel better soon, Mrs. Honeyman."

Sébastien made a gagging motion behind his back. Olivia giggled.

"Look, Grandma, we made you breakfast," Alex said in a cheery voice. He placed the tray on her lap.

"See, Grandma?" Olivia said. "It's *Painterman Eggs.* Remember when we named them? I know you love them."

Grandma looked at the tray and then at the children. "That's so thoughtful of you" She sounded on the verge of tears. "But I'm just not hungry."

"But Grandma, you've got to eat," Claire said. "Please."

Grandma hesitated. She took a piece of toast, broke the yolk, and dipped the toast in. She ate a bite.

"Is it good, Grandma?" Olivia asked.

Grandma nodded. She took another bite, then put the toast down. "That's enough."

"But –" Sébastien began.

"Really, it was delicious," she said, "but I just can't eat any more."

Both eggs and all but one little strip of toast were still on the plate.

Grandma slid down in the bed and closed her eyes.

They returned to the kitchen and dished out the remaining eggs and toast. But not even Olivia felt like painting any golden designs on her plate.

SIX

IT'S AN EMERGENCY!

No one said it out loud. There was no discussion. But after that, everyone gave up. They couldn't find the deed, they couldn't cheer Grandma up, so what was the point? Alex and Claire went fishing, Geneviève disappeared somewhere, presumably to meet Shane, Olivia went up to Hugh's Perch with her paints, and Eve and Charlie explored the island. That left Sébastien. He curled up with one of Grandpa's secret code books and spent an enjoyable afternoon trying to decipher scrambled messages. When he got stumped and was tempted to look up the answers, he heard Grandpa's voice in his head: *No peeking!* With a rueful smile, he resisted – and managed to solve five out of seven codes. But he missed Grandpa more than ever.

—•

That evening, after a delicious dinner of fresh trout, caught by Alex and Claire, and a salad, picked from Grandma's garden – another dinner that Grandma didn't come down for – Claire said, "What's for dessert?"

Eve shrugged. "There're some peaches."

Claire rolled her eyes. "*Mo-om.* I mean *dessert.*"

"Did you finish those ca –" Alex began, until Claire kicked him under the table. Eve was strict with the amount of sugar she allowed her children, and she didn't need to know about those two candy bars.

"We need something sweet," Claire said. Then, before her mother could object, she said, "Hey! That's the trouble with Grandma."

"What is?" Olivia said.

"We haven't made her any dessert. I bet if we did, she'd eat it up. And she'd feel better."

"Nice try, Claire," Geneviève teased.

"No, really, I bet something sweet would pick Grandma right up."

"And send her through the roof with a sugar rush," Eve said.

"Come on, Mom," Claire said. When Eve refused to agree, Claire slid her chair close to Charlie's and leaned, puppy-like, against his shoulder. "Wouldn't you like a nice little something with your coffee, Charlie?"

"Well, now that you mention it . . ."

"See, Mom?" Claire said.

Eve shook her head. "It's too hot to start baking."

Claire knew she had her. When her mom started bringing in the feeble, second-line excuses, the game was over.

"We don't have to bake. I know just the thing," she said.

"What?"

"*Emergency Fudge,*" Claire said triumphantly.

"Claire, that's solid sugar!" her mother objected.

"But it's quick. And you don't have to bake it. And Grandma loves it." *And it just happens to be my favorite thing in the world,* she added mentally.

"You've got to promise to have just one little piece,"

Eve said. "I don't want to be peeling you off the ceiling all night."

"Yay!"

Emergency Fudge
A strong beacon in an emergency

Ingredients:
1/4 cup butter
1/4 cup water
3 cups icing sugar
1/2 cup instant nonfat dry milk
1/2 cup cocoa powder
pinch salt
1 teaspoon vanilla

Optional: 1/2 cup pecans, chopped

Instructions:
1. Butter a 9"x5" loaf pan. Set aside.
2. In a medium-sized saucepan, melt the butter and water.
3. In a bowl, mix the icing sugar, milk powder, cocoa, and salt. Add half of the butter mixture to the dry ingredients and mix well, then slowly add the second half, beating constantly with a wooden spoon.
4. Add the vanilla, and the pecans if desired.
5. Pour the mixture into the prepared pan. Cover and refrigerate until firm, about 30 minutes. Remove from fridge and cut into squares.

Although Geneviève was disappointed that they had all the ingredients on hand, everyone else was delighted. The fudge went together quickly, and in five minutes they were turning the mixture into the pan.

They all gazed at the shiny brown slab as Claire lifted a knife.

"Wait," Geneviève said. "We're supposed to refrigerate it for thirty minutes."

"But this is an emergency!" Claire said. "See?" She pointed to the caption under the title. "That's why it's called *Emergency Fudge.* It's for when you need a sugar fix and you can't wait."

"It is not," Geneviève said, playfully smacking her sister on the head. "It's from the olden days. For when you had unexpected company and you needed to whip something up in a hurry. Grandma told me."

"That's not Grandma's writing, it's Grandpa's," Sébastien said. "Why does he keep scribbling these things on Grandma's recipes?"

"Who cares?" Claire said. "Let's dig in."

"It'll be crumbly," Gen warned.

"I love crumbly!" Claire cried.

Everyone laughed, and Geneviève gave in with a shrug. Claire cut the fudge into squares, and they each took one. Geneviève was right. The fudge crumbled to pieces in Claire's hands, but somehow scooping up all the little bits with her tongue only made them seem more delicious.

"Look at you," Alex said, laughing at Claire's chocolate-smeared mouth.

Claire didn't care. She refused to wash her hands until she had licked every last smidge of chocolate off them.

"Whew!" Olivia said, downing a glass of water. "That stuff *is* sweet."

"I know," Claire said, looking longingly at the remaining fudge.

"Hey," Sébastien said, "I thought this was for Grandma."

"Oh, yeah," Claire said. "I mean, of course it is."

But once again, Grandma wasn't interested. She appreciated all the children's efforts, she said, but she just wasn't hungry. They weren't to worry, she wasn't starving, she told them, pointing to an empty teacup and a mostly eaten piece of toast. She just had no appetite for more than that. Too many worries.

They trooped downstairs. While Claire nibbled away at the fudge, Sébastien stared at the words scrawled on the recipe card. The note wasn't just an idle thought, he was sure of it. It had to mean something. But what?

He fetched the other two recipes and spread them all out on the kitchen table.

The keystone is the key.

Are you feeling artistic this morning?

A strong beacon in an emergency.

What was Grandpa getting at? Keystone . . . key . . . artistic . . . beacon . . . emergency . . . Nothing fit together. Nothing made sense. Yet he was sure that this was some kind of message from Grandpa.

"What are you doing, Seb?" Alex said.

"Trying to figure out what Grandpa's saying with these little notes."

"That again?" Geneviève rolled her eyes.

"It could mean something!" Sébastien said heatedly. "Grandpa always left messages in strange places."

"Yeah, but he was probably just having fun. Leaving little love notes for Grandma."

Sébastien shook his head. "There's more to it. They're connected in some way. I just don't know how."

"The great sleuth," Geneviève said. "You win that big science prize at school and you think you're Sherlock Holmes or something."

"I do not!"

"What science prize?" Olivia asked. "You didn't tell us, Seb."

"It was nothing," he said, blushing. "Never mind."

There was a moan from across the table. Claire's hand was over her mouth. "I don't feel good."

The others looked at the fudge tray. There were only a few crumbs left. "Claire! Did you eat all of that?" Alex asked in disbelief.

Claire nodded, turning pale. "I need a bathroom." She ran from the room.

"And it's an emergency," Geneviève couldn't resist adding.

Several minutes later, Claire came back in. "Remind me never to eat *Emergency Fudge* again."

"Like that'll work," Sébastien said.

Even Claire managed a smile. Soon after, everyone went up to bed. But Sébastien sat with the three recipes, trying to figure out what the messages could mean. His mind skittered around uselessly.

Then he had a thought.

He raced upstairs and tapped lightly on Grandma's door. If she was asleep, he wouldn't bother her.

"Yes?" she called.

Sébastien peeked in. "Can I ask you something, Grandma?"

"Of course, sweetheart."

He showed her the three recipes. "We found these notes from Grandpa. Do you have any idea what he means?"

Grandma stared. She reached out and touched Grandpa's handwriting. Then she burst into tears. "Oh, Sam . . . Sam . . ."

"Grandma, I'm sorry," Sébastien said, alarmed. "Please don't cry –"

Eve ran into the room. "Mom! Are you okay?"

Grandma just sobbed.

Eve turned to Sébastien. "What did you do?"

Sébastien felt his face grow warm. "I didn't mean . . . I just showed her . . ."

There was the patter of footsteps on the stairs, and Geneviève raced in. "What's the matter, Grandma –"

She caught sight of the recipes in her brother's hand. "Sébastien! Of all the –"

"I'm really sorry, Grandma," Sébastien said, feeling wretched. "I didn't mean to upset you."

Grandma moaned helplessly.

"It's okay, Mom, it's okay . . ." Eve crooned, patting her mother on the back. Over her shoulder, she said, "Go."

Pushing past Geneviève, Sébastien went downstairs. He put the recipes away. By the time he climbed heavily back upstairs, Grandma's room was quiet.

SEVEN

KNITTING A RIDDLE

"Now what?" Claire said the next morning. "Well, if Sébastien hadn't gone and made things worse –" Geneviève began.

"I didn't mean to!"

"Gen, that doesn't help," Alex said, shooting Seb a sympathetic look.

"The only thing I can think of," Olivia said, "is, remember when Muriel said she had something for us from Grandpa? And that it could help Grandma? Maybe we should go get it."

"Good idea, Liv," Alex said, brightening. "Maybe it'll give us a clue about the deed."

They all hopped on their bikes and headed toward town. Riding down the road, Claire noticed short wooden posts sticking up out of the ground, with little red ribbons tied around their tops. She slowed to a stop. "What are those?"

The others coasted to a stop beside her. "Survey stakes," Sébastien said.

"What does that mean?"

"It means that Tantalus is planning where they're putting the road to the mine."

They gazed at the line of stakes stretching into the distance, imagining huge trucks and machines roaring down this quiet country road. They rode on in silence.

When they arrived at the general store, Muriel greeted

them with a laugh. "This is getting to be a habit. What are you kids cooking today?"

"Actually, nothing, Muriel," Alex said. "Remember you said you had something for us from Grandpa? We thought we'd pick it up."

"Right!" Muriel said. "I keep forgetting to drop it off. Let's go." She hung a BACK SOON sign in the window, and they set off down the road. Her house was only a short distance away, beside a large berry patch overlooking the south shore.

Muriel led them into the kitchen, which smelled deliciously of berries. A few dozen jars of preserves stood on racks on the counter: pink raspberry, purple blackberry, red strawberry.

"Here, take this for your grandma," Muriel said, handing Geneviève a jar of raspberry jam. "Maybe it'll bring back her appetite."

Olivia was standing there, gazing at the jars. "Muriel," she said in a hushed voice, "could I come over and paint those sometime?"

Muriel followed her gaze. "Sure, anytime." She patted Olivia's arm. "Now then, where did I put that thing?"

She rummaged around in a few cupboards before feeling on top of the cabinet where she kept her knitting yarn. "Aha!" she shouted and reached down a long, very thin package wrapped in brown paper. "Who wants to do the honors?"

When no one answered, Geneviève said, "I will." She tore open the paper and held out – a knitting needle. One knitting needle. She shook out the paper, looking for the other needle, but there was none.

"One knitting needle?" Sébastien said. "That's it?"

"That's it," Geneviève said.

Alex looked at Muriel, puzzled. "And Grandpa said this could help Grandma?"

"'This can help Lily if need be,'" Muriel said. "Those were his exact words."

"Do you have any idea what he meant, Muriel?" Sébastien asked.

Muriel shook her head. "I'm as stumped as you are."

"Look at this," Olivia said. She was pointing to the thick end of the knitting needle. Wrapped tightly around it was a length of clear thread, and dangling from the thread was a small tag with the number 6 on it.

The others drew closer. "That's fishing line," Claire said. "Right, Alex?"

"Right."

"One knitting needle, fishing line, number 6," Sébastien said. "What on earth could Grandpa have meant?"

"I wish I could help you, but I have no idea," Muriel said, "and I'd better be getting back to the store."

The cousins walked back to where they'd left their bikes. "I hate to say it," Geneviève began, climbing onto her seat, "but is it possible that, at the end, Grandpa was . . . well, a little soft in the head?"

"No!" Sébastien shouted.

The others looked at him in surprise.

"He wasn't," Sébastien insisted. "He was doing puzzles. He was reading. He was as sharp as ever. Right?" He appealed to the others.

"I don't remember," Claire said sadly.

"Seb's right," Olivia said. "He wasn't loopy."

Sébastien shot her a grateful look.

"Well, I wish he'd given us a clue," Geneviève said. She put the jam and the knitting needle, rewrapped in the paper, in her basket. They rode silently home.

Eve had no idea what the knitting needle was for, and, after the upset of the night before, everyone was afraid to ask Grandma if she did. Geneviève rolled it up in the brown paper and put it in the pantry, along with Grandma's recipes.

—•—

After everyone went off in different directions, Sébastien sat and thought about the knitting needle. Somehow he knew it was connected to the deed, though he couldn't imagine how. Grandpa wouldn't have done something so odd without a good reason. And he knew that Grandpa hadn't been crazy. Sick, yes. In pain, yes. But his mind had been clear right up until the end.

Sébastien listed everything he knew about the knitting needle. Grandpa had left it with Muriel. There had to be a reason for that. He'd attached a number to it. There had to be a reason for that too. But what?

That line of thought was getting him nowhere.

Okay, he said to himself. Grandpa wrote notes on certain recipes. There was something about the recipes. Could there be a connection between the knitting needle and the recipes?

Once again, Sébastien dug out the three recipes they'd tried so far. But none of them had anything to do with a knitting needle, or knitting, or yarn. Or anything!

He flopped down with a sigh.

Maybe it was a different recipe, he thought. Maybe the knitting needle had something to do with another recipe. A recipe of Muriel's. His mouth watered thinking of *Muriel's*

Berry Pandowdy. His favorite dessert. It was so good, with the warm berries and the biscuity topping. Mmm . . .

He pulled himself back. Grandma must have dozens of Muriel's recipes in her collection. Finding the right one – if there *was* a right one – was going to be like finding a needle in a haystack. *Needle! Groan!*

He hauled out the notebooks and boxes and envelopes.

Muriel's Blueberry Muffins. No message from Grandpa.

Muriel's Blackberry Pie. No message.

Muriel's Raspberry Tarts. That one had a note in Grandma's writing that said, "Reduce fat. Don't over bake!" Nothing from Grandpa.

Muriel's Triple Berry Jelly.

Muriel's Strawberry-Rhubarb Crumble. That one had a bunch of jottings in Grandma's handwriting. For the amount of sugar, she'd crossed out "¼ cup" and scribbled "⅓ cup," and she'd written "Add pinch of nutmeg."

Muriel's Raspberry Scones.

Cripes, how many recipes were there?

Muriel's Berry Compote.

Muriel's Blackberry Crisp.

Why did Muriel have to be such a good cook?

He was down to the last notebook. He flipped through the pages. And there it was – right in his favorite!

Muriel's Berry Pandowdy

Don't needle me. Get to the point!

Ingredients:
2 1/2 cups blueberries

2 1/2 cups blackberries
1/2 of a lemon
1/3 cup + 2 tablespoons sugar
1 1/2 cups + 2 tablespoons flour
2 teaspoons baking powder
1/4 cup + 3 tablespoons cold butter, cut into cubes, plus extra for the dish
10 tablespoons whipping cream + 1 tablespoon for top

Instructions:
1. Preheat oven to 375°.
2. Butter a medium-sized glass or ceramic casserole dish.
3. Squeeze the juice from the half lemon. Toss berries with the lemon juice, 1/3 cup of sugar, and 2 tablespoons of flour. Spread in bottom of baking dish.
4. In a separate bowl, mix the 1 1/2 cups of flour with the baking powder, remaining 2 tablespoons of sugar, and salt. Add the cold, cubed butter and mix, rubbing between your fingers until the butter is mostly incorporated into the flour and the largest pieces of butter are the size of peas.
5. Add the whipping cream and mix with a wooden spoon just until the dough comes together.
6. Drop pieces of dough onto berries and brush each piece of dough with the extra cream. Bake until the biscuit topping is golden and dry to the touch, and the berries are starting to bubble up, approximately 40 minutes.

7. Cool at least 30 minutes before serving - berry
juices will be very hot! Serve with whipped cream
or vanilla ice cream.

Sébastien jumped up with a whoop. *Don't needle me!*
There was a link! And he'd found it! And Grandpa wasn't
crazy. And neither was he.

He sat down abruptly. There was a link between the
message on the recipe and the knitting needle. So could there
be a connection between the other messages and some other
objects? Was that what Grandpa was trying to show them?

He grabbed the three other recipes.

The keystone is the key.

What was a keystone? Sébastien knew he'd heard of it before,
but he couldn't remember what it was. He started pacing. He
could hear Grandpa's voice in his memory, explaining. "And
the keystone is . . ." What? *Think!*

More pacing.

"And the keystone is the focal point at the center of the
design . . ."

Agh! What was it?

"All the other stones radiate out from the keystone . . ."

Grandma's herb garden! That was it!

Sébastien ran outside. Sure enough, beneath Grandma's
herb pots was the circle of flagstones. And the rosy one in the
center, he now remembered Grandpa telling him, was called the
keystone, because it was the one that all the others fitted around.

The keystone is the key.

What was Grandpa saying? It sounded like they were supposed to find a key – but where?

Moving all the herb pots aside, he noticed something odd. Although all the other flagstones were cemented together, the keystone was not. There was a thin space all around it. Sandy soil showed through from below.

Sébastien fetched a crowbar, levered up one end of the keystone, and peered beneath it. At first, all he could see were shadows and dirt. But then . . . something silver. Was that a box? Twisting, he grabbed the thing and placed it to the side. Carefully, he lowered the keystone back into place.

He lifted the box. It was about the size of a bar of soap. The outside was completely covered in duct tape. Heart pounding, he stared at it. Then he ran inside. He cut away the duct tape to find a plastic box. Inside that was another, smaller, box, and inside that were several layers of plastic bags, each sealed with duct tape. Finally, he came to one more very small plastic box. He opened it and parted a mound of lambswool. Something nestled inside the wool gave off a goldish glint. Reaching into the mound, Seb pulled out –

"A key!" he shouted.

Just like with the knitting needle, there was a length of fishing line looped through the hole. The tag that dangled from the line said 7.

He shrieked with laughter. *Leave it to Grandpa. A key under the keystone!*

Sébastien stopped dead. This key must unlock the place where the deed was hidden! "The key, the key, the key!" he yelled, laughing, jumping up and down.

Just then the others came home.

"Sébastien!" Alex said. "What on earth are you –"

"The key! The keystone! The knitting needle! The recipes!"

"Are you cracked? What are you talking about?"

Stumbling over his words, Sébastien told them what he'd figured out, how the knitting needle had led him to *Muriel's Berry Pandowdy*, and how he'd then realized that the other notes must be linked to other objects, and how he'd remembered about the keystone and dug up the box and – "Here it is!"

"Here what is?" Claire asked.

"The key that must unlock the place where the deed is!" Geneviève said, understanding flashing over her face. "Let's find it!"

They ran from room to room, trying the key in every lock they could find. But it didn't fit into the front door or the back door of the cottage. Nor did it unlock the drawer in Grandpa's desk, or Grandma's jewelry box, or Grandpa's toolbox, or the old trunk in the living room where Grandma kept spare blankets. It didn't unlock the cabinet in Grandma's studio, where she kept her cans of turpentine. It didn't fit a padlock Alex found in a kitchen drawer or the door to the pantry or an old bike lock lying on the deck or the door to an antique cupboard in the living room.

It didn't unlock anything.

Dejected, they headed back to the kitchen.

"Now what?" Claire said, flopping onto a chair.

"I'm sure that's the key to where the deed is hidden," Geneviève said. "We just have to find the right door."

Sébastien shook his head. "That might be the right key, but I have a feeling Grandpa wanted us to keep looking for something else. After all, the tag says number 7. There must be other things that come first."

"Like the knitting needle. That's number 6," Olivia said.

"Right," Sébastien said. "Grandpa wrote notes on other recipes. I think that's what we have to figure out – what the notes mean."

"Why bother?" Geneviève said. "We've got the key. Looking for other clues is a waste of time. Everything isn't a detective game, Seb."

"It's not a game. I want to find the deed as much as you do. I just think –"

Geneviève stood up. "I'm going to search for the door."

"Where?" Alex said.

"On the property. Around the island. Anywhere I can think of. Who's coming with me?"

Claire and Alex jumped up. Sébastien and Olivia stayed where they were.

—●—

Marching down the deck steps with the key in hand and Claire and Alex trailing behind her, Geneviève was sure she'd find the lock and prove Sébastien wrong. He always thought he knew everything. Not this time.

"Let's try the boat shed," she said cheerfully. "You know how Grandpa loved boating."

Claire, full of new energy, bounded ahead. "Race you!" she called to Alex, then laughed as he grabbed her arm and pulled her back. They arrived together in a spray of sand.

The key didn't fit the boat-shed lock.

It didn't fit Grandpa's tackle box, which, as Claire pointed out, he never locked anyway.

It didn't fit a padlock fastened to a rusting bike that no one could remember anyone ever riding.

"Okay," Geneviève said, her confidence dampening. "Um . . . the garden shed?"

No.

"The mailbox!"

No.

"This is no fun," Claire grumbled.

Geneviève agreed, though she didn't say so.

"Come on," she called, "we can't give up. Maybe it's somewhere else on the island. Let's try Mrs. Hedberg's."

Dragging along behind, Claire and Alex followed her down the road to Grandma's next-door neighbor's house. They explained about the deed, and, with Mrs. Hedberg's permission, tried the key in various locks.

But it didn't fit Mrs. Hedberg's front door. Or her back door. Or her barn door. Or her garden shed door or her tool shed door or her buffet or her desk.

Standing outside Mrs. Hedberg's house, Geneviève slumped. All they'd managed to accomplish for their trouble was to get dusty and tired and thirsty.

The three of them trudged home.

EIGHT

SEARCHLIGHT

Geneviève, Claire, and Alex found Sébastien and Olivia at the kitchen table, giggling and talking excitedly.

Sébastien looked up. Seeing Geneviève's face, he didn't ask if they'd had any luck.

Olivia said, "Look! Seb and I figured out the next clue. It's a paintbrush!" She pushed forward the *Painterman Eggs* recipe. "Grandpa's clue, *Are you feeling artistic this morning?*, was talking about a paintbrush." She held up one of Grandma's paintbrushes. Tied around the handle was a length of fishing line, with a tag labeled 2.

"Cool!" Alex said. "Good work."

Geneviève sat down heavily and put the key on the table. "So now we have a key, a knitting needle, and a paintbrush. What on earth are we supposed to do with them?"

"No idea," Sébastien said cheerfully. "But I'm pretty sure they have something to do with finding the deed."

"That's crazy," Geneviève said. "Now I'm not even sure if the key has anything to do with the deed. It seems like a dead end. Maybe these things are just clues from some old scavenger hunt Grandpa dreamed up one time. We could be totally wasting our time."

"I don't think so. I think the notes have a purpose. Why else would the objects be numbered?"

"So you would know when you had found all the things in the scavenger hunt and could win a prize," Geneviève said sarcastically.

"Look, Gen, if you don't want to help, don't," Sébastien said. "But Olivia and I are trying to figure out what the note on the *Emergency Fudge* recipe means."

Geneviève flushed, but she didn't leave.

Sébastien pushed the recipe into the middle of the table. "A strong beacon in an emergency," he read. "Any ideas?"

"Well, a beacon is like a signal," Alex said.

"Or a light," Olivia added. "Like in a lighthouse."

"We can hardly collect a lighthouse," Geneviève said.

"How about 'emergency'?" Sébastien asked.

Olivia started sketching. Looking over her shoulder, Sébastien watched as she drew a rectangle that turned into an ambulance. She drew the light on top, with lines twirling out from it to suggest flashing beams of light.

Picking up on Olivia's thought, Sébastien brainstormed. "Ambulance . . . hospital . . . doctor . . . accident . . ." His voice trailed off. He huffed in frustration.

"Forget the ambulance," Alex said. "Where would you go if you had an emergency?"

"The Emergency Station," Sébastien and Geneviève said at once.

"I said it first," Gen said.

"I did," Seb said.

"Guys!" Alex said. "All right, let's go to the Emergency Station and see if there's a clue hidden there for us."

"That's ridiculous," Geneviève said.

Laughing, Claire said, "He left us a knitting needle at Muriel's. How ridiculous is that?"

—•—

They laid their bikes on the grass next to a small building on a spit of land that formed one side of Otter Bay. A sign over the door said OTTER ISLAND EMERGENCY STATION. Next door to the station, on the other side of a hedge of flowering bushes, was Wilensky Air, the float-plane company owned by "the mayor." Part of the Wilensky Air office now sported a sign saying TANTALUS MINING. On the other side of the Emergency Station was the First Aid Clinic, and then a row of shops, ending in the ferry dock, which formed the other end of Otter Bay.

The cousins went into the Emergency Station. Floor-to-ceiling shelves held everything needed to respond to a boating emergency: lifejackets, lanterns, coils of rope, first aid kits, flashlights, water bottles, blankets. A rowboat with oars was suspended on a frame near the rear double doors. Out those doors, a short path led to the lighthouse, where a light twirled continuously.

Kevin was sitting behind a desk. He looked surprised to see them. "Hi, kids. What can I do for you?"

"Um . . . we're looking for something," Sébastien asked.

Kevin looked expectant, as if waiting for him to continue. When he didn't, Kevin said, "Anything in particular?"

The cousins exchanged glances. "We think so . . ." Alex said carefully, ". . . but we don't know what it is."

"Huh?"

"Did you know our grandpa?" Sébastien said.

"Sam?" Kevin broke into a grin. "Of course. Good man."

"Do you know if he . . . um . . . left something here for us?"

Kevin cast his eyes aside as if trying to think. "Not that I know of," he said finally. "But I do remember he was in here one day helping me do inventory, and he was fussing around over there." He pointed to a stack of shelves that held blankets, bottles of water, and flashlights.

"Thanks!" Geneviève said, and they hurried over. She stood on a chair and started unfolding and refolding blankets. Claire and Olivia peered between the rows of water bottles on the bottom shelf. Sébastien and Alex started examining each flashlight.

"Nothing here," Claire said, straightening up.

"Or here," Geneviève said, climbing down.

"Or – wait!" Sébastien said. "Alex, do you see this?" He pulled out a flashlight from the back of the row. Alex held his thumb up. The others pressed close.

"What? I don't see anything," Olivia said.

Sébastien pointed to a slender, nearly invisible thread tied around the handle of the flashlight. "Fishing line," he said. He held up the tag. "Number 4."

"Go, Grandpa!" Claire yelled, and they all laughed.

Sébastien took the flashlight over to the desk. "Kevin? Could we borrow this for a while? We promise to bring it back."

Smiling, Kevin cocked his head. "You wouldn't want to tell me what this is about, would you?"

"We're not even sure ourselves," Claire told him.

"But we think it's going to stop those mining people from getting their hands on Grandma's cottage," Sébastien said.

An angry look crossed Kevin's face. "In that case, keep it as long as you like. Anything to stop those —" He gritted his teeth as if swallowing back a bad word. " — those people."

Thanking him, they left the Emergency Station and walked over to where they'd left their bikes.

"Seb, I thought you were nuts when you said those things had something to do with the deed," Alex said, lifting his bike, "but now I'm beginning to think —"

He stopped abruptly as Sébastien clasped his arm.

"What?"

"Sh." Sébastien pointed with his head. "Look who's there."

The children peered through the bushes. Coming out of Wilensky Air were Stan Wilensky, Mark Saxby, the mining company guy — and Charlie.

NINE

A TRAITOR IN OUR MIDST

"What's he doing here?" Geneviève whispered. "I thought he and Mom were at Hugh's."

"That's what I'd like to know," Sébastien whispered back. Putting his finger to his lips, he motioned them all closer to the bushes.

The three men stood at the end of the walkway, chatting.

". . . too much opposition from the locals?" Mark Saxby was saying.

"No worries," Stan Wilensky said in his booming voice. "We'll take care of that."

They missed the first part of what Charlie said. ". . . plans moving along for the access road?"

"Yes, indeed, as soon as we secure the last few properties," Mark Saxby answered.

The cousins exchanged a furious look.

Peering through the leaves, Sébastien saw Mark Saxby reach into his briefcase and hand Charlie a stack of booklets. "Here you go," he said. "These should come in handy."

There was the sudden roar of a float plane approaching the island. Growing louder as it taxied to the dock behind Wilensky Air, it drowned out the men's conversation. They leaned close and spoke into one another's ears. Then they shook hands and parted, Stan Wilensky and Mark Saxby strolling toward a coffee shop on the other side of the office, Charlie walking to his car, which the cousins now saw was parked down the street. He drove away.

The children turned to face each other.

"I can't believe it," Claire said, a sick look on her face.

I can, Sébastien was about to say, but just then the float-plane engine went silent, and an idea struck. "Wait here," he said. "Be right back."

"Seb!" Alex said. "Where are you going?"

"To have a look around Wilensky Air."

"You can't just barge in there," Geneviève said.

"I'm not," Sébastien said with a grin. "I'm going to sneak in. If they come back before I'm out, send me the signal."

Claire nodded. The signal when they were little, and hadn't wanted their parents to catch them doing something forbidden, was to caw like a crow.

Sébastien went around behind Wilensky Air. The float plane was now moored to the dock, and a young man, his arms laden with a stack of cardboard boxes, was approaching the back door of the building.

Sébastien sprinted to the door and held it open.

"Thanks, pal," the man said.

Sébastien followed him inside.

"Delivery for Tantalus Mining," the man said to a secretary, who had come into the back room.

"Oh," she said, looking flustered. "Mr. Saxby's at coffee. Well, just put them in there." She pointed to a room across the hall from the main office of Wilensky Air. TANTALUS MINING said a plaque on the door.

Sébastien opened the door and stood aside. With a grunt, the delivery man dropped the boxes on the floor, then went back out for another load.

Sébastien stayed put. He looked around. It looked like an ordinary office: desk, computer, shelves, phone. Display panels were stacked against the wall.

Nothing unusual. Nothing that wouldn't be found in any business office. Of course, Sébastien had no idea what he was looking for.

He wandered over to the bookcase. There were stacks of booklets, all bearing the company's lake-and-mountain logo. Sébastien recognized the one that Valerie London had shown at the open house, OTTER ISLAND TANTALUM MINE: ECONOMIC REPORT. He took one. Then he saw another pile: OTTER ISLAND TANTALUM MINE: ENVIRONMENTAL REPORT. That was the one that Wayne Cheng had presented. The one that there were no copies of at the open house. Sébastien took a copy of that one too. He stuffed them under his shirt, just as the delivery man came in with another load of boxes.

—●—

Anxiously, Claire peered through the bushes, around the back of the building, through the bushes again. Where was Seb? What was taking him so long? The two men would probably be back soon and –

Two sets of pant legs approached along the sidewalk. Careful not to be seen over the top of the hedge, Claire raised herself up and peeked. Stan Wilensky and Mark Saxby were strolling back, chatting, coffee cups in hand.

She elbowed Geneviève, who alerted Alex and Olivia.

"What do we do?" Olivia mouthed.

The two men drew closer. ". . . profits should be excellent," Wilensky was saying.

"Yes, indeed, and there's plenty of interest from investors," Saxby replied.

They turned down the walkway to Wilensky Air.

Claire squatted there, frozen. Then she opened her mouth wide. "Caw! Caw!"

Inside, Sébastien heard the call. *Oh, no!* He had to get out now. He dropped to the floor, hoping that the front counter would block him from the view of anyone coming in the front door, and started crawling toward the back door.

Claire watched in horror as the two men continued down the front walk. She had no way of knowing if Sébastien had heard her warning, but there was no sign of him yet. And if he came running out now, the two men would see him. She was furious with him for taking such chances, but she couldn't let him get caught. What could she do?

Wilensky and Saxby started climbing the three short stairs to the Wilensky Air office.

Claire threw herself on the ground. "Caw, caw! Cough, cough! Ack, ack!" she yelled, clutching her throat.

"Claire, what are you doing?" Geneviève whispered, grabbing her arm.

Claire continued choking. "Agh, agh! Help!"

The two men hurried back and peered over the bushes. "What is it? What's the matter?" Wilensky asked.

"Help! she's choking!" Geneviève called. Claire faced away and coughed hard.

"One minute, be right there," Saxby said. "Hang on, kid."

He and Wilensky ran around the hedge and knelt beside Claire. By this time, the cousins had clued in to what she was doing. They squatted beside her, patting her on the back.

Wilensky helped Claire sit up. He slapped her on the back. "What happened?"

"She swallowed something," Geneviève offered.

"Well, just cough it up, that's it," Saxby said, stretching Claire's arms overhead. "Big cough. There you go."

Claire gave a mighty hack. "Whew! I think that got it – whatever it was."

Out of the corner of her eye, she saw Sébastien peeking out from around the back of the building.

Saxby and Wilensky helped Claire stand up. Wilensky continued to pat her on the back. "Are you all right now?"

"Oh, much better." She smiled weakly at her two saviors. "Thank you so much! I don't know what I would have done without you."

"Not at all," Saxby said. "Just glad you're okay."

The two men retrieved their coffee cups and walked back around the hedge to the Wilensky Air entrance.

As soon as they were out of sight, Sébastien darted from the back of the building. He hugged his sister. "Good show, Claire!"

She turned furious eyes on him. "Where the heck were you?"

"Just looking around. I didn't think they'd come back so soon."

"You gave us a heart attack!"

Sébastien gave an abashed smile. "Sorry. But what an act, Claire! You sounded totally real."

She grinned. "I was good, wasn't I?"

"So?" Alex said. "Find anything?"

Sébastien pulled the two booklets out from under his shirt.

"That's all?" Geneviève said. "Just some booklets?"

Sébastien pointed to the environmental report. "This is the report they didn't have at the open house the other day. There could be something in it that they don't want us to see."

"That looks like the pile of booklets he gave Charlie," Olivia said.

At Charlie's name, everyone went silent. They exchanged uncomfortable glances.

"I can't believe it," Geneviève said.

Sébastien shook his head. "I knew there was something about him."

"But he's so nice," Geneviève wailed.

Sébastien snorted. "He sure got you and Claire believing that."

"Do you suppose he's getting money from them?" Alex asked.

"Of course. Why else would he do it?"

"Should we tell Aunt Eve?" Olivia asked.

"Oh, poor Mom!" Geneviève burst out. "She finally meets a nice guy –"

"Nice! He's stabbing her in the back," Sébastien said. "Of course we tell her. She's got to find out – the sooner, the better."

"No," Claire said. "What if we're wrong? What if Charlie really isn't in with them?"

"Yeah, he was just being friendly with those guys," Sébastien said sarcastically.

"We don't know for sure," Claire insisted.

"Oh, grow up!" Sébastien said. "You always think the best of everybody."

"And you always think the worst," she shot back.

"It *did* look bad," Olivia said. "But why don't we wait? There's no harm if we keep it to ourselves a little longer."

"Yeah. Maybe we'll find out it wasn't what it looked like," Alex said.

Sébastien rolled his eyes. "And in the meantime, Charlie gets to keep plotting with those creeps."

"I'm with Olivia," Geneviève said. "I can't bear the thought of telling Mom. Or Grandma."

"Me too," Claire said.

"And me," Alex said.

All eyes turned to Sébastien. "All right, I'm outvoted." He kicked the ground in disgust. "You guys just don't want to face facts."

He jumped on his bike and started pedaling.

—●—

When they got home, Eve and Charlie were sitting on the deck, tall glasses of iced tea in front of them.

"Where were you?" Eve said. "We got back early, and I was looking to see if you wanted to go for a swim while Charlie ran some errands."

Errands, right, Sébastien thought.

"At the Emergency Station," Geneviève said.

Sébastien watched Charlie as his sister said this. Charlie's cheeks colored. *Gotcha!* Sébastien thought.

"The Emergency Station?" Eve repeated. "Is everything okay?"

"Everything's fine," Alex said. "We found this." He held up the flashlight.

Eve and Charlie looked puzzled. Sébastien didn't want to talk about what they'd been up to in front of Charlie, but there didn't seem to be any way to get rid of him, so he explained about the clues in the recipes. Claire fetched the other objects to show them.

"But what are the numbers for?" Charlie asked. "And what are you supposed to do with them?"

"We have no idea," Sébastien said. "But I'm sure they have something to do with the deed."

"You think your grandfather planted a bunch of clues in Lily's recipes, which are supposed to lead to these things, which are supposed to lead you to the deed? That's crazy," Charlie said.

"You didn't know Grandpa!" Sébastien shouted.

"Sébastien!" Eve said. She turned to Charlie. "I know it sounds farfetched, but it *is* the kind of thing he might have done."

"If only we knew what to do with this stuff," Alex said.

"What if we showed it to Grandma? Do you think she'd know, Mom?" Claire asked.

Eve shook her head. "It upset her so much to see Grandpa's handwriting the other day, I don't want to do it again. See if you can figure it out without bothering her."

"We'll try," Sébastien said. "We've got to find the deed before Tantalus, *and their friends*" – he looked straight at Charlie – "start building the mine."

TEN

UNDER THE MAGNIFYING GLASS

That evening, Geneviève curled up on the couch and texted back and forth with Shane; Olivia went into Grandma's studio to paint; and Sébastien, Claire, Alex, Eve, and Charlie gathered in the kitchen for a game of Monopoly. As usual, Sébastien landed in Jail on his first turn, and, as usual, Claire landed on Boardwalk and promptly bought it. Then Alex ended up in Jail with Sébastien.

"We might as well just stay in here," Sébastien told his cousin. "Claire's going to win anyway."

Rattling the dice, Claire grinned. "This is the only thing I'm smarter at than you, Seb."

She wasn't the only one who had luck, though. Charlie scooped up Park Place and then a succession of railroads. Eve, who had no properties, put her arms around him. "You wouldn't want to slip me one of your houses, would you, sweetheart?"

The others laughed, but Charlie just gave a weak smile.

That wasn't the only odd thing about Charlie, Sébastien noticed. On her next turn, Claire landed on Park Place. With a groan, she started counting out money, preparing to pay Charlie rent. But Charlie didn't ask for any. Claire waited. But when Charlie remained silent, staring off into space, she flashed a sly smile at the others and handed the dice to Alex.

And the next time it was Charlie's turn, he sat there with the dice in his hand until Eve poked him.

"Sorry," he said with a sheepish smile. "Guess I was somewhere else."

Thinking about the mine, Sébastien thought, *and how he's going to help his new buddies put it through.*

Finally, after Claire won, bankrupting Sébastien, Eve, and Alex, they put the board away.

Charlie stood up and stretched. "I think I'll go for a walk," he said.

"I'll come with you," Eve said, reaching for her sweatshirt.

Charlie hesitated. "Uh . . . I'd rather be by myself, if you don't mind."

Eve looked surprised. "Are you all right, Charlie?"

"Yeah, I just . . . I'll be back soon."

Charlie picked up a flashlight and left. A moment later, Eve headed upstairs to bed. As soon as she was gone, Sébastien said to Alex and Claire, "Come on, let's find out what Charlie's up to."

"How do you know he's up to something?" Alex said.

"You saw how weird he was!"

"You're so suspicious, Seb," Claire said. "He probably just wants to look at the stars."

"Yeah, and he was probably just shooting the breeze with those guys today," Sébastien said sarcastically. He tugged on a baseball cap. "You coming or not?"

"Coming, coming!" Claire said, as she and Alex followed Sébastien outside.

There was no moon, but in the wash of light from the cottage windows, they could see Charlie on the sand below the deck. Standing there, he looked left, right, then headed down the beach to the right, toward the boat shed.

"What's he doing?" Claire whispered. "Taking out a canoe at this time of night?"

"Hush!" Sébastien said.

Hugging the shadows against the dark side of the cottage, he led them across the deck. As silently as they could, they jumped down onto the sand. Charlie paused, cocking his head as if he'd heard something. They froze. Charlie continued walking down the beach.

Running in spurts, staying in dark patches, the three cousins advanced to the dock, crouching in the shadows beneath, and then to Grandpa's canoe, where they hid along its length. Charlie, twenty feet away, stopped again. They held their breath. He walked around to the far side of the boat shed. They heard a click, then saw a brightening on the ground where the flashlight beam must be shining.

"What on earth is he doing?" Alex said in a low voice.

"Let's go see," Sébastien whispered.

Tiptoeing on the sand, they made their way to the near side of the boat shed. Sébastien heard a page being turned. Followed by his cousin and sister, he edged along the wall of the shed until he could peer around the corner.

Charlie was sitting on the sand. The OTTER ISLAND TAN-TALUM MINE: ENVIRONMENTAL REPORT was spread out on his lap, and in the light of the flashlight beam, he was looking at it with a magnifying glass. Every so often he turned the page and changed the position of the magnifying glass, the flashlight beam skittering over the sand until he focused it once more.

Sébastien raised his eyebrows at Claire and Alex. "See?" he mouthed at them.

Abruptly there was the beep of a telephone keypad being dialed. From their position just around the corner, the cousins could hear the phone ring on the other end.

"Hi," Charlie said. "I've been looking at the report . . . Yeah, a really positive environmental message . . ."

Sébastien's heart beat faster. Who was Charlie talking to? Someone he was trying to interest in the mine? Another traitor, selling out another family?

"Can't tell . . . ," Charlie said, ". . . says it's a green project . . . fantastic profits too . . ."

Sébastien squeezed Alex's shoulder.

"Yeah . . . I'll keep looking . . . keep you posted . . . okay, 'bye."

There was the click of the call being ended, then the sound of Charlie standing up and brushing the sand off his pants.

"Come on!" Alex mouthed, motioning for them to get out of there fast.

Scampering across the sand, they ran for Grandpa's canoe. A moment later, the flashlight played over their backs.

"Hey," Charlie yelled, "what are you guys doing out here?"

"Charlie!" Claire said, turning with a smile. "What a surprise!"

By this time Charlie had caught up with them. "What are you doing?" he asked again.

"Um . . ." Sébastien's mind raced. Quickly he reached down and scooped up a seashell. "Gathering seashells . . . for my collection. You get the best ones at night, you know. They wash up in the tide."

Beside him, he heard Alex stifle a snort.

Charlie looked at Sébastien oddly over the flashlight beam. "I didn't know you had a seashell collection."

"You didn't?" Alex said. "Oh, yeah, Seb's been into seashells from way back."

"Take this one. It's a *Cypraea bistrinotata*." Holding out the specimen he'd just picked up, Sébastien thanked his photographic memory for bringing back a Latin name from a book on shells he'd once read. He had no idea if this shell was actually a *Cypraea bistrinotata,* but it sounded good.

Charlie looked impressed. "You'll have to show me your collection sometime, Seb."

"Sure thing, Charlie."

"Well, it's late. Better head back now," Charlie said.

The cousins had no choice but to fall into line with him. As they walked back up to the cottage, Sébastien elbowed Claire, but she refused to look at him. He groaned with frustration. What was it going to take for Claire to admit that Charlie was in with Tantalus up to his neck?

ELEVEN

TWINKLE, TWINKLE, LITTLE STAR

The next morning all five cousins hauled Grandma's recipes out of the pantry and started looking for more of Grandpa's notes, hoping that they would lead to more objects.

"Here's one!" Olivia said.

Everyone leaned over to see. *Would you pare a pair if I said a prayer* Grandpa had written on the recipe for *Pear Crisp*.

"A pair of what?" Claire said. "Shoes?"

"Socks?" Olivia guessed.

"Pants?" Alex said.

They tiptoed upstairs and, while Grandma slept, silently searched the closet where Grandpa's clothes used to hang. Nothing was hidden there.

"Maybe he means a paring knife," Geneviève said. But a search of the utensil drawer turned up nothing.

"You know," Sébastien said, reading the notation again, "I think he's just making a joke. You know, pare, pair, pear. Just having fun with the words."

"I suppose so," Alex said with a sigh.

They went back to shuffling pages.

A few minutes later, Claire gave a shriek. "I've got one!"

It was in the recipe for *Chocolate Cinnamon Sparkle Cookies*.

Grandpa had written, "Star light, star bright, can you see the sparkle tonight?"

"My favorite!" Geneviève said. "Yum."

"What does it mean?" Olivia said, reading the note.

"Something about stars," Alex said. "And someplace where you can see them."

"That could be the dock," Claire said. "We used to lie out on the dock and look at the stars sometimes."

"But where on the dock would Grandpa put something?" Geneviève asked. "Wouldn't it get wet? Or wash away?"

"One way to find out," Claire said. She dashed outside, and the others followed. But a careful examination of the underside of the dock showed nothing.

Back inside, they all stared at the note. No one could figure out what it meant.

"You know what I think?" Geneviève said. "I think we should make the cookies. Maybe we'll figure it out while we're making them."

"There isn't time," Sébastien said. "We've got to get on with finding the clues."

"I know . . . but I really think baking them might help."

"You just want an excuse to go back to the general store," Sébastien said.

"I do not!" Geneviève said, blushing.

"Yeah, right," Sébastien said.

In the end, no one had a better idea, so they set off for the general store.

———●———

He was there. No matter that Sébastien brushed by him

without saying a word. No matter that even Alex said "*Ge-en*" in an annoyed tone when he saw him waiting out front of Muriel's store.

All that mattered was that Shane was there and that he blazed that smile at her and touched her arm as they went inside.

"You up for more cooking?" Geneviève said.

"Wouldn't miss it," he whispered. "Maybe this time I can help you figure out the clue."

"Would you?" she asked.

His smile was the answer.

She was diverted, though, by a loud "Oh, no!" coming from Muriel. Along with her cousins, Geneviève hurried over to the cash register, where Chad and Rachel were placing their groceries.

"What's the matter?" she asked.

"The Wongs gave in. They've decided to sell," Muriel told them.

Geneviève didn't have to be told what bad news that was. One by one, Tantalus was picking off the islanders. No doubt they were counting on the fact that, as more people went along with the mine, the last few holdouts would feel obliged to sell too.

Ringing up Rachel and Chad's purchases, Muriel wagged her finger at them. "They'll redouble the pressure on you next."

"We know," Chad said in a worried voice.

"We'll try to hold out," Rachel said. "Oh, if only we could start our business and get some money coming in!"

The cousins picked up the bittersweet chocolate, butter,

and almonds they needed, and rode home, each of them thinking about the bad news.

Chocolate Cinnamon Sparkle Cookies

Star light, star bright, can you see the sparkle tonight?

Ingredients:

9 ounces (approximately 1 3/4 cups) bittersweet chocolate

3 tablespoons unsalted butter, cut into cubes

2 eggs

1/2 cup granulated sugar, plus 1 cup more for rolling

1 tablespoon honey

1/4 cup finely ground almonds or almond meal

1 tablespoon cocoa powder

1 teaspoon cinnamon

Instructions:

1. Chop chocolate, then set aside 1/4 cup. Fill a small pot halfway with water and bring to a simmer. Transfer remaining chocolate to a heat-proof bowl, then place bowl on top of simmering water. Stir the chocolate gently until it melts. Add cubes of butter and stir until they melt. Once all the butter and chocolate have melted, set the mixture aside to cool while you prepare the other ingredients.

2. Beat the eggs, sugar, and honey until the mixture thickens. The eggs are ready when you can lift the whisk and the mixture holds a ribbon-like shape

when you dribble it back on itself.

3. Gently stir the chocolate mixture into the egg mixture, then add the ground almonds, cocoa, salt, 1/2 teaspoon of the cinnamon, and the chocolate you set aside earlier.

4. Cover the dough with plastic wrap and chill it until it is firm enough to roll, at least 4 hours or overnight.

5. Preheat the oven to 325°.

6. Prepare a bowl with 1 cup of granulated sugar and the other 1/2 teaspoon of cinnamon. Roll the chilled dough between your palms into 1 1/4" balls, and drop the balls into the sugar.

7. Gently shake the bowl to coat cookie balls with sugar, then place on a lined or buttered baking tray 2 inches apart.

8. Bake cookies until the tops are dry but the centers are still soft, about 12 minutes.

9. Remove cookies from oven and cool 15 minutes, then gently drop the cookies (round side down) into the remaining sugar to add more sparkle.

The cookies came together quickly, and, after the cousins waited impatiently for the dough to chill, the kitchen filled with a delicious chocolatey, cinnamon smell as they baked. When Geneviève took the trays out of the oven, Claire said, "Look! They sparkle!" She smacked her head. "So *that's* why they're called *Sparkle Cookies!*"

Everyone laughed.

Several glasses of milk later, two racks of cookies had

disappeared.

"Well, Gen, any ideas?" Sébastien said.

"Oh, yeah," Geneviève said, looking embarrassed. "Hmm . . . okay, let's see . . . *Can you see the sparkle tonight?* Um . . ."

"I have an idea," Shane said.

Geneviève turned to him, eyes alight. "Really? What?"

"Well, you know how sometimes the ocean glows at night with a kind of yellow-green neon light?"

"Bioluminescence," Sébastien said. "It's actually a chemical reaction that produces light in certain sea creatures."

"Sébastien!" Geneviève said. "Stop showing off."

"No, it's cool," Shane said. "That's what I meant. So maybe your grandpa meant that kind of sparkle."

"But how would we ever find something in the water?" Olivia said.

"Or are we supposed to catch one of the sea creatures?" Alex said. "Grandpa wouldn't want us to do that."

Shane shrugged. "Don't know. Maybe I'm wrong."

"No, no," Geneviève said quickly. "It's a great idea."

"But we'll have to wait for dark," Sébastien said.

"No problem with that," Geneviève said, blushing.

◆━━

All evening, the five of them plus Shane – who stayed for dinner – waited for it to get dark. Finally, the sky turned deep blue . . . then inky blue . . . then black.

Geneviève took Shane's hand and skipped outside. The others followed. Alex led the group to a place on the beach, to the left of the dock, that sometimes had that bioluminescent glow. But there was no glow tonight, just the normal reflection of the waves in the starlight.

"Maybe if we walk a little farther," Shane said. "I could have sworn I saw it around here when I was on a boat one night."

They walked on, but still found nothing. Then they headed back the other way, to the far side of the boat shed. Nothing. Just ordinary, night-dark water.

"No glow. No sparkle. No nothing," Sébastien said.

"And even if we did see the glow, how could we find anything?" Olivia said. "Are we supposed to dive under and feel on the bottom? Grandpa would never expect us to do such a dumb thing."

"Liv!" Geneviève said. She turned to Shane. "Sorry."

"She's right," Sébastien said angrily. "And now we've wasted a whole day waiting for nothing."

"No, I'm sorry," Shane said, sounding contrite. "I just thought . . . well, I was just trying to help."

"You did help," Geneviève said fiercely. "Don't listen to them."

"Maybe I got the place wrong," Shane said. "Maybe if we walk in that direction –"

"Forget it," Sébastien said.

"Seb!" Geneviève hissed.

A car pulled up beside the house, its headlights illuminating the deck and Grandma's garden.

"That's my mom," Shane said, and sprinted toward the car. "Good luck," he called over his shoulder.

When he was gone, Geneviève turned toward Sébastien and Olivia. "How could you!"

"How could *we?*" Sébastien repeated. "*He's* the one who

steered us wrong."

"It was just an innocent mistake," Geneviève said.

"Oh yeah?" Sébastien shot back.

Gen put her hands on her hips. "What's *that* supposed to mean?"

"Nothing," Sébastien muttered. But he didn't think it was nothing. He had a funny feeling that Shane had suggested the bioluminescence on purpose, to distract them. But why?

"Now he probably hates me," Geneviève went on. "Thanks a lot!"

"Listen, Gen, I'm sorry if I was rude, but it was a stupid idea," Olivia said.

"He was just trying to help."

"It's our thing, Gen, not his –" Sébastien began.

"Who cares? We need all the help we can get. The clock's ticking, if you hadn't noticed."

"I've noticed!"

"Then stop acting like a jealous baby."

"I'm not jealous! You shouldn't be letting a stranger into our family business."

"What, you think he's a spy or something?" Geneviève's voice rose. "You're pathetic!"

"I am not! You're the one –"

The kitchen door opened and a pool of light streamed out. "Kids!" Eve bellowed. "Inside. Now!"

Geneviève turned and ran.

Claire and Alex walked silently after her.

Olivia hung back with Sébastien. "I'm with you, Seb," she said in a low voice. "I don't trust him either."

TWELVE

"A BOON TO THE ISLAND"

"Grandma?" Alex said softly, opening the door a crack.

Grandma turned. Her hair was flattened against the pillow. Her skin was almost as pale as the sheets on her bed. Alex had the horrifying thought that if they didn't find the deed, Grandma would just fade until she was taken away along with the cottage.

"Yes, sweetheart?" Even her voice sounded weak.

"Could we show you something?"

Grandma nodded, and the cousins entered the room, all walking carefully, as if afraid to make a loud noise. Alex held the four objects behind his back.

"Now, Grandma, these things are from Grandpa, and if you don't want to look at them, you don't have to," he began. "But we think they have something to do with the deed. And we need your help to figure it out."

"Let me see."

Alex placed the paintbrush, the flashlight, the knitting needle, and the key on her lap. She took in a sharp breath, and her eyes filled with tears. Alex was afraid she was going to start crying, but she didn't. She picked up the paintbrush, looked at the number on the tag, and laid it down again. She touched each of the other objects. "Tell me," she said. Her voice trembled, but she didn't cry.

And so they did – interrupting each other, backing up, and starting over to explain the confusing bits.

Tears rolled down Grandma's cheeks as she listened. But, to Alex's surprise, when they'd finished, she only sighed and said, "Oh, Sam, you dear, crazy man," in a fond voice.

"Do you have any idea what these things are for, Grandma?" he asked.

"None." She sighed. "Oh, if only I could remember what he said. It's there . . ." She touched her head. "I can hear his voice . . . but then it's gone."

"I think maybe we can find the deed anyway, Grandma," Sébastien said.

"Really? How?" For the first time, her voice held a spark of life.

"Well, I'm pretty sure the objects have something to do with it," Sébastien said. "I think Grandpa put clues in the recipes so we would find these things, and he wanted us to do something with them. I just don't know what."

Grandma pushed herself up to a sitting position. "You know," she said, "now that you mention it, I think Sam did say something about recipes. I was so confused at the time, I can't remember exactly what he said, but I'm pretty sure . . ." She leaned forward, and there was a glint in her eyes that the children hadn't seen since they'd arrived at the cottage. "Do you think . . . is it possible that these objects are leading to where the deed is hidden? That it's some kind of puzzle that Sam set up?"

"That's exactly what we think, Grandma," Olivia said.

"So . . . ," Grandma said, her voice sounding more excited, "if you find them all . . . they might reveal the hiding place?"

"Right!" Claire said. She started bouncing up and down on her toes.

Grandma actually smiled. "Then there's hope after all!"

"Yes," Sébastien said. "And we found another one of those notes, and we think it's a clue, but we don't know what Grandpa is talking about. Would you . . . take a look?"

Grandma nodded, and Alex handed her the recipe card.

Grandma grinned. "Hugh's Perch, of course. Grandpa and Hugh used to stargaze up there all the time. Said it was the best place on the island to see the stars."

"Grandma, you're brilliant," Claire said.

"Let's go ask Hugh if he knows anything about this," Alex said, and they started for the door.

"Wait," Grandma said. "First, help me out of bed."

"Yay!"

—•

Bearing the tin of cookies, the cousins made their way to Hugh's place along a trail that skirted the beach. At first the only sounds were the hush of the waves, the squawks of gulls, and the hoot of a far-off ferry horn. But as they drew closer, they began to hear voices. Angry voices. They looked at one another and hurried on. Coming around the bend of the driveway, they saw Hugh and his son Ted standing nose to nose – two tall, thin, scarecrow-like men, one bald and one with bristly blond hair. Hugh was waving a newspaper around.

"Good for the island?" he sputtered. "How can you believe such rubbish, let alone print it?"

"It's not rubbish, Dad! You just –" He cut off abruptly as the cousins came into view.

Hugh's gaunt face brightened for a moment. "Hi, kids." Then it drooped again. "Did you see the snow job my son published in the local rag?"

"It's not a snow job!" Ted said. "I keep telling you –"

"And I keep telling you, you're wrong!" Hugh thundered. He turned to the cousins. "Listen to this headline: MINE WILL BE A BOON TO ISLAND. What a crock!"

"What's a boon?" Claire asked.

"It means something good," Sébastien explained. "Like a big benefit."

Rattling the paper, Hugh read aloud, "'At a recent open house held at Otter Island Community Hall, Tantalus Mining president Mark Saxby said the proposed tantalum mine will make Otter Island an important player in the worldwide telecommunications industry. Saxby said the mine will bring jobs, economic development, and better roads to Otter Island.' Sure – jobs for Tantalus and their cronies, wrecking the island!"

"That's not true," Ted began, but Hugh cut him off and continued reading.

"'We're delighted to partner with Tantalus Mining in this exciting new venture,' said Stan Wilensky, owner of Wilensky Air and a community leader. "'Islanders will benefit from economic development and investment opportunities.'"

"What's that supposed to mean?" Olivia asked.

"It means Wilensky's going to make a pile of money from the mine," Hugh said.

"Dad, I keep telling you, Stan's a good man. He's trying to move the island forward –"

Hugh waved his hand and continued, "'Company scientist Dr. Wayne Cheng outlined the stringent environmental precautions Tantalus Mining is taking to protect the pristine environment around the mine site.'" Hugh slammed his fist against the paper. "Stringent, my foot! You think salmon are going to swim up those poisoned streams?"

"They're not going to be poisoned," Ted said. "The environmental report showed that. And so does this." He pulled a slip of paper from his pocket and handed it to Hugh.

Hugh read aloud, "'The Otter Island tantalum mine is green! It will be great for the environment! Full speed ahead on this exciting mine project that promises fantastic profits while protecting fish, birds, and wildlife!'" He looked at Ted. "Where did this come from?"

Ted shrugged. "Someone mailed it to me at the *Observer* office. I don't know who. But obviously they agree with Tantalus."

"No doubt some crony they paid to spout this poppycock."

Hugh handed the paper back to Ted, but Ted shook his head. "I don't need it."

"Can I have it?" Sébastien asked.

"Sure," Ted said, giving it to him. "Look, Dad," he went on, "you may not like my position on the mine, but I've done my research –"

"Spoon-fed by that London woman," Hugh shot back.

Ted blushed, and Sébastien remembered seeing him in conversation with Valerie London, eagerly writing down whatever she was telling him.

"Yes, I got information from Tantalus," Ted admitted. "But I've read the reports, seen the studies. They're sound."

Hugh threw the newspaper on the ground. "If you believe those so-called reports, then you haven't got the brains I gave you credit for."

"That's it, Dad!" Ted said. Scooping up the newspaper, he stalked off to his car. "I'll talk to you when you're through insulting me." He slammed the car door and drove away.

Watching the dust from Ted's wheels rise and swirl, Hugh's shoulders slumped. "Sorry, kids. Didn't mean to put you through that. I just –" He sighed. "Sorry."

"It's okay, Hugh," Alex told him.

They stood in silence.

Finally, Geneviève said, "We made you some cookies, Hugh."

"You did?" A smile lit his gaunt face. "A man can't think gloomy thoughts when he's eating cookies. Come in and share them with me."

"We will. But first, is it okay if we poke around the Perch a bit?"

Hugh looked perplexed. "Sure. You don't have to ask, you know that. But whatever for?"

"Well . . . ," Gen said, "we don't know. We think Grandpa hid something up there for us."

"On the Perch?"

Alex showed Hugh the clue and explained about the deed and the objects they'd found so far. "So we're pretty sure he means the Perch," Alex concluded.

"Must do," Hugh said thoughtfully. "You know, I seem to remember Sam messing around up there before he – well, before he got real bad. Didn't tell me what he was doing, but he said if his grandkids came by, tell 'em to look up at the stars."

"Look up at the stars?" Olivia repeated.

Hugh nodded. "To be honest, I thought he'd gone a little

soft in the head, from the cancer and all, and didn't pay it any mind. But maybe he did put something up there for you."

The trail up to the Perch crossed behind Hugh's garden, switched back beneath the crest of the cliff, and circled through a grassy meadow, rising steadily until it ended on a high bluff. It commanded a spectacular view westward, overlooking Hugh's place below, Grandma's cottage and dock to the left, a rocky beach to the right, and the sparkling sea in all directions. On a clear day, like today, you could see neighboring Heron Island, crowned by the tall cedars where the birds loved to nest.

Huffing, Geneviève put her hands on her hips and looked around. The top of the Perch was slate, spotted with bunches of wispy, seed-topped grass in places where soil had managed to gain a toehold. There were some boulders that made excellent seats for stargazing, and the odd windswept snowberry bush, its branches curving away from the sea. That was it. "Now what?" she wailed. "There's nothing up here."

"Wait a minute," Hugh said. "Maybe Sam didn't mean right here. After all, he said to look up at the stars, didn't he?"

He started walking down the Perch in the opposite direction from which they'd come. The cousins shot each other confused looks, but after a moment Geneviève knew where Hugh was headed. On the east side of the cliff, away from the wind, Hugh had built a shed. It was where he kept his telescope.

Can you see the sparkle tonight? the clue said.

"Tell them to look up at the stars," Grandpa had told Hugh.

Geneviève quickened her pace, and the others must have clued in, too, because they nearly tumbled in on her heels when Hugh opened the door.

The shed was small and dark. Hugh lifted the cloth that covered the telescope and peered underneath, but nothing was hidden there. The cousins crawled around on the floor and poked into corners, bumping into one another and getting dusty.

Claire sighed. "Another dead end –"

"Wait!" Geneviève said. "What's that?"

She was pointing to a wooden post that framed one corner of the shed. There was a gap of a few inches between the top of the post and the roof, and there seemed to be a small package wedged into the gap.

Hugh managed to reach the package and handed it to Geneviève. It was a plastic box, similar to the one that had held the key buried under the keystone. She opened it, unwrapped the layers of tape, smaller boxes, more tape, and cotton.

She held up a glass object that was suspended from a loop of fishing line. The glass was the size of a small plum and shaped like a teardrop. Its sides were chiseled so that they broke the surface into many planes. Even in the dim light of the shed, the glass cast moving rainbows of light on the floor and walls as it turned.

"What is it?" Claire asked.

"A prism," Geneviève replied.

"It's beautiful," Olivia said, her gaze following the splashes of light.

Geneviève held up the tag dangling from the fishing line. "Number 5," she said.

"A flashlight, a paintbrush, a knitting needle, a prism, and a key. What on earth was Grandpa trying to tell us?" Alex said.

No one had an answer. In silence, they watched the beam of light flash and turn, flash and turn.

THIRTEEN

A STAKE THROUGH THE HEART

Grandma got dressed. She ate a whole muffin and drank a whole pot of tea – at the kitchen table. The next day, she put on her apron and made French toast for breakfast – her famous French toast with a dash of nutmeg, a dusting of icing sugar, and fresh sliced strawberries. The day after that, she went into the studio.

When she came out with blue spots in her hair, the rest of the family high-fived each other. "Grandma's back!" they cheered.

———

A couple of days after the visit to Hugh, Sébastien sat at Grandpa's desk, looking at the two reports he'd stolen from the Tantalus Mining office. Both were full of fancy looking graphs, glossy photos of scenic island spots, and phrases printed in large letters that said things like CUTTING-EDGE SCIENCE! and PRESERVING PRISTINE ISLAND BEAUTY.

He flipped through the economic report first, but found only the same information that Valerie London had presented at the open house: the graph showing all the money that would flow to the island, the list of jobs that would be created, the chart showing how valuable tantalum was.

He turned to the environmental report. Again, he saw

exactly what had been in Wayne Cheng's slides: the same reassuring information about the "temporary, sustainable, state-of-the-art containment system," the same message about "how little impact the mine would have" on the island's fish and wildlife. There didn't seem to be anything new or controversial. So why had he, Sébastien, gotten the idea that the Tantalus folks hadn't wanted people to see the report?

He remembered the slip of paper Ted had given him, and pulled it out of his pocket. It was a computer printout. It said:

The Ott**er Island** tantalu**m** **m**ine **is** gr**een! It w**ill **be gr**eat **f**or th**e** **e**nvironment! Full **s**peed a**h**ead on **t**his exc**it**ing **m**ine **pro**ject **t**hat **pro**mises fantastic **pro**fits **wh**ile **p**rotecting **fi**sh, **b**irds, and **w**ildlife!

That was all. Why, he wondered, would these sentences be written on a slip of paper? Could they have been from an early draft of the report? He flipped back through the booklet. He didn't find that exact passage anywhere, though bits of it – "great for the environment," "exciting mine project," "fantastic profits," "protecting fish, birds, and wildlife" – appeared on different pages.

Sébastien looked at the paper more carefully and noticed that it was printed in a mix of regular and bold letters. That was odd. Why would it be like that?

He went downstairs to find Olivia. She was sitting on the deck floor, sketchpad resting on her knees, drawing Claire's bike, which lay on its side on the sand. Seb stood silently and watched as her eyes flicked up, down, up, down, her pencil constantly moving. It was as if her eye and hand were connected, two parts of the same limb. He peered over her shoulder. Olivia was shadowing the edge of the bike tire, making it look as though the bike had just been thrown down and the tire was still spinning. Amazing.

"Liv?"

"Yeah?" Eyes still on the bike.

"Would you look at something?" When she nodded, he handed her the slip of paper. "Why is some of this text plain and some in bold?"

Olivia pushed her glasses up on her nose and examined the paper. She shrugged. "Sloppy design job, I guess." She snorted. "I could do better than this."

"Why would they print it like that? What's the point?"

Olivia shook her head. "In a rush, maybe?"

"Maybe," Sébastien echoed. But something told him there was more to it than that.

He went back upstairs and stared at the paragraph. There didn't seem to be any pattern to the bold and plain letters: Sometimes the bold letter appeared at the beginning of a word, sometimes in the middle, sometimes at the end. There would be a stretch of several plain letters, then two or three bold letters in a row. Some of the bold letters were capitals, but most were lowercase.

What possible reason could there be for writing the sentences so that some letters jumped out at you and other letters didn't?

Could it be, he wondered, that the differently written letters, when put together, spelled out a secret, some kind of message that only some people were supposed to know? Like a secret code?

Sébastien grabbed a piece of paper and wrote down the bold letters in order.

tIadmmigeItwbgeafeeotlsehedhi tnmirjetprisiptshpefbiswd

He looked at the list. Written like that, the letters sure didn't spell out anything that made sense. He could pull out a few smaller words from the string of letters: ad, fee, hit, jet, sip. But they didn't say anything.

What if he rearranged the letters? Maybe that was the trick. He started scrambling letters and jotting down words. He came up with *age, feet, steal, hope, fill, heat, reason, head, hide, neat, road, foal, dish, jeep, read, ape, prison.*

He sighed. None of those conveyed a message.

So maybe the secret was in the plain, unbolded letters. He started copying these into a much longer list.

TheOtersIntantaluinesrenillertor thnvirnmenFulpedaaontisexcigne pocthatomsefantastcrofiwilerotcti ngishrdandillife

Taken .together, they were gobbledygook. Reading in order, he could form smaller words: *The, tan, ant, ill, men, on, sex, that, hat, rot, tin, and, life.*

He could form words by mixing up the letters: *heart, thin, nest, vine, full, excite, path, fantastic, file, hard, tone, demand, remain, flog, reap, sleet, grow, sandy, minced, poor, mention, spell, while, newsreel.*

So what? None of those said anything. If they spelled out a secret message, he sure couldn't see it. He threw down his pencil. Maybe he was wrong. Maybe there was no secret message and he was just imagining things. So why was he so bothered by it?

Just then, a loud rumble from outside broke his thoughts.

—•—

Kicking a soccer ball back to Claire, Alex heard a loud noise. A Tantalus Mining truck was coming up the driveway.

Shouting for the others to come, he ran to the studio to fetch Grandma. Red-tipped paintbrush in hand, she hurried outside with him just as Sébastien barreled down from upstairs.

Four workers, two men and two women, all wearing baseball caps bearing the familiar lake-and-mountain logo, were setting up tripods. One pair set their tripod up on the shoulder of the driveway beside the cottage, while the other moved into the beach grass on the seaward side. They started looking through viewfinders.

Grandma waved her paintbrush. "Excuse me. Just what do you think you're doing?"

Whew, Alex thought. He hadn't been sure if the "real" Grandma was back, or if the sad, weak one was still around.

A fifth person climbed out of the truck with a clipboard under his arm. He strolled over with a pleasant smile. "Good afternoon, ma'am. We're the Tantalus Mining survey crew, and we're here to survey for the access road to the mine."

"I never gave anyone permission to tramp around my property," Grandma said.

"With respect, ma'am, we don't need permission. Tantalus has an agreement with the Otter Island road commission to do the survey."

"You can't do that!" Grandma said, but no sooner were the words out of her mouth than one of the surveyors pulled a wooden stake out of a pouch on his work belt and started pounding it into the ground about twenty feet to the seaward side of the driveway.

"Get off my land!" Grandma said, pointing with the paintbrush.

Way to go, Grandma, Alex thought.

"I'm sorry, ma'am, but we have a job to do. We'll be out of your way just as soon as we can."

With a tip of his cap, he strode off to join his colleagues. Meanwhile, two more stakes, each one some distance from the road, were pounded in. Their red plastic ribbons fluttered in the breeze.

Grandma walked over to the man with the clipboard. "I'm not going to sell. You're wasting your time."

"Our orders are to survey for the entire road, just in case, ma'am."

Grandma squared her shoulders. "I'm going to call the police if you're not out of here in two minutes."

The young man smiled. "Good thing we're just finishing up, then." And in fact, Alex saw, the crew members were folding up their tripods. As they filed back to the truck, they kept their eyes straight ahead. The man raised a hand. "Good afternoon, ma'am, kids. Have a nice day."

As the truck disappeared around the bend, Grandma's shoulders sagged. "What am I going to do?" She sounded weak and scared now, not at all like the warrior who'd just yelled at the surveyors.

"Don't worry, Grandma, it'll be okay," Alex said. But even he wasn't sure his words were true. What could they do – what could anyone do – when the company just marched in like that?

"I can't lose this place," Grandma said, tears beginning to roll down her cheeks. "Oh, if only I could remember what Sam said. It's on the tip of my tongue – but every time I try to remember, it's gone."

"Don't cry, Grandma," Olivia said, squeezing her hand. "We'll find the deed."

"I have to prove this place is mine. I have to!" Grandma wiped her face with her shirt hem. She took a deep breath. A steely look passed over her face. "Come on," she said, "it's time to search the recipes."

FOURTEEN

KABOOM!

Grandma cleaned her paintbrush, and they all sat down at the kitchen table with the recipes. Looking through them seemed to lift her spirits. She chuckled, pointing to *Homemade Whole Wheat Noodles with Peanut Butter Sauce*. "What a disaster that was! Grandpa loved pasta and he loved peanut butter, so I decided to make up a recipe putting the two of them together. The noodles were thick and heavy. The sauce was gloppy and lumpy. Grandpa took a bite, and he chewed . . . and chewed . . . and chewed . . . Later I tried feeding the mess to Mrs. Hedberg's sheep, and even they wouldn't eat it!"

Everybody laughed.

They paged through the recipes. Geneviève got excited when she found a note in Grandpa's writing in the recipe for *Quince Paste* that said Sourpuss!, but Grandma explained that that was just a reference to Hilda Schultz, from whom they'd bought the quinces. "Eve was just a little baby then. So adorable, with her sticking-up black hair and big round eyes. I asked Mrs. Schultz to hold her for a minute while I got out the money, and Eve threw up on her." The grandchildren hooted. "She charged us extra for dry cleaning – and she was only wearing a ratty old shirt anyway."

They continued turning the pages.

The sound of car tires approached the cottage. Everyone looked up.

"Not them again!" Grandma said, alarmed.

But it wasn't the Tantalus truck. It was a small blue car that no one recognized. Everyone went outside in time to see Rachel and Chad climb out.

They've come to tell Grandma they're selling, Sébastien thought, his heart sinking.

"Oh, Lily, look at your garden," Rachel said, walking across the deck. "What a marvelous green thumb you have."

Sucking up isn't going to soften the blow, Sébastien thought.

"I'm afraid it's been rather neglected lately," Grandma said. "But nothing can stop zucchini! Please, take some home." She picked them a bag full and then invited them into the living room. The cousins trailed behind curiously.

"Here, let me make tea," Grandma began, but Chad waved his hand.

"No, Lily, please don't bother. We just came over to borrow a recipe."

There was a pause. "A recipe?"

"Yes," Rachel said. "We've got a big crowd coming over this weekend – it's Chad's birthday in two days –"

"Happy birthday, Chad," Grandma said.

"Thanks."

"I was trying to think what to make, and I remembered that *Brown Sugar Spice Cake* of yours," Rachel continued. "It's so delicious, and I know it would go over great. So I wondered if we could copy down the recipe."

Silence.

"Lily?" Chad said. "If you'd rather not give it out, we'll understand –"

"No, no, it's fine," Grandma said. "It just took me by surprise, that's all. Recipes have been . . . well, in our thoughts lately, shall we say. Come into the kitchen."

Sébastien's mind started racing. Did Rachel and Chad really just want the recipe? Or was that just a ploy to get to see all of Grandma's recipes? They had said they were thinking about selling out to Tantalus. Could they secretly be on the mining company's side? Could they have somehow found out what the key recipe was – the one that would lead to the deed?

Grandma, Rachel, and Chad sat down at the table, and the others clustered around. Sébastien decided to watch Rachel and Chad closely.

"Oh my, would you look at this collection!" Rachel said, picking up the worn black binder. "Isn't it amazing, Chad?"

Chad nodded. "Very impressive."

While Grandma flipped through the file box, trying to remember where she kept the spice cake recipe, Rachel started turning the pages. "Just think – you've made every one of these!"

Chad looked intently over her shoulder.

They're checking them out, Sébastien thought, *looking for the secret recipe.*

"Not in here," Grandma said, puzzled. "Maybe it's in one of these envelopes."

While she continued looking, Rachel flipped through the recipes in the manila folder. "Look, Chad, *Grilled Tomatoes with Feta and Basil.* We could do that with our basil . . . Oh, *Scallop Stew* – that sounds yummy."

"Hey, not so fast," Chad said, putting his hand on Rachel's to stop her from turning the page. "What's that one? *Chocolate-Ginger Cupcakes.* Now, that's unusual, isn't it? You don't often hear those two flavors going together."

They're stalling, Sébastien thought. *Searching.*

Or, what if this is just a decoy? What if Brown Sugar Spice Cake *really* is *the recipe they want, and they're just pointing out these other ones to throw us off?*

"I invented those cupcakes," Grandma said proudly. "Sam always said I could make money if I baked them commercially, but I wasn't interested. I'd rather have time to paint . . . and garden."

"With a beautiful spot like this to live in, who wouldn't?" Chad said, looking out the kitchen window.

Finally, Grandma pulled a sheet of paper out of the folder. "Here it is! Gee, I haven't made this in a long time. Maybe I will."

"Good idea, Grandma," Claire said, licking her lips.

Rachel copied out the recipe. "We really must be running. Got to get ready for the big crowd. Thanks a million, Lily."

"Not at all," Grandma said. "Any time."

After they left, Grandma went for a nap. Sébastien turned to the others. "Don't you think there was something funny about Rachel and Chad?"

"Like what?" Claire asked.

"Why were they so interested in *Brown Sugar Spice Cake?*" Sébastien said.

Geneviève rolled her eyes. "Duh. Because they want to make it for their party."

"Maybe not."

"Sébastien, what are you talking about?"

"Maybe they know something. Maybe that recipe is the key to the deed. Maybe they want to find it before we do."

"What!" all the others said at once.

Sébastien blushed. Okay, it sounded pretty silly now that he said it out loud . . . but there still might be something to it.

"Look, we know they're thinking about selling their property to Tantalus."

"Yeah. So?" Alex said.

"Well, maybe they're actually on their side. Maybe they want the mine to go through."

"But we heard them say they don't want to sell," Olivia said.

"But maybe that was just a line. And if they do want the mine to go through, they don't want Grandma to find her deed because it would make the project go easier without all these people holding out. And if they know something about that recipe, then they might find the deed before we do."

Geneviève corkscrewed her finger beside her head. "You've really done it now, Seb. First you suspect Charlie. Then Shane. Now Chad and Rachel. You're paranoid!"

"It does sound pretty far-fetched, Seb," Alex said, looking at him with pity.

"Then why did they come over here to get the recipe, when they could have just looked on the Internet for one like it?" Sébastien replied. "And why did they go through the recipes like they were searching for something?"

"Now that you put it that way . . ." Olivia began.

"Liv!" Geneviève cried. "Not you too."

Olivia shrugged. "It sounds crazy . . . but when Seb explains it, I can't help but wonder. What if they *do* know something? What if they *are* working against us?"

Geneviève rolled her eyes. "Okay, you great detectives, let's suppose just for a moment – which I don't believe at all, but let's just suppose – that Seb's right. Then what? What do we do?"

"Well . . . we could try making that recipe and see what happens," Sébastien said.

"But we're supposed to be looking for clues, not making *Brown Sugar Spice Cake*," Alex said.

"But we need to beat them!" Sébastien said. "We can't let them figure it out first."

"I don't believe this," Geneviève said. "The survey stakes are up. The mine is getting closer. And you want to waste time making some copycat recipe? You're the one who flipped out because Shane 'wasted our time' looking for that glowing stuff in the water!"

"He did waste our time," Sébastien said under his breath.

"Forget it. I'm not making some cake just because Sébastien has a wild idea about Rachel and Chad." Geneviève left the kitchen.

Claire shook her head and followed. Alex did the same, giving Sébastien a sorry look.

Brown Sugar Spice Cake

Ingredients:
4 1/4 cups cake and pastry (or all purpose) flour
2 teaspoons baking powder

1 1/2 teaspoons baking soda
1 teaspoon salt
1 teaspoon cinnamon
1/4 teaspoon nutmeg
1/4 teaspoon allspice
zest of 1 lemon (finely shaved peel)
2 cups brown sugar
1 cup vegetable oil
2 teaspoons vanilla
4 eggs
2 cups buttermilk

Instructions:

1. Preheat oven to 350°.
2. Sift flour, baking powder, baking soda, salt, cinnamon, nutmeg, and allspice. Set aside.
3. Beat the brown sugar, lemon zest, vegetable oil, and vanilla. Add the eggs, one at a time, beating well between each addition. The batter will thicken and start to lighten in color. Beat for 1 minute once all eggs have been added.
4. Add the dry ingredients in 3 additions, alternating with the buttermilk and finishing with an addition of dry ingredients. Scrape down sides of bowl between each addition. Beat lightly for 30 seconds after last addition of dry ingredients.
5. Butter two 9" cake pans, then dust with flour, tapping out extra. Scrape batter into pans, and bake until a skewer inserted into center of each cake comes out clean and surface of cakes springs

back lightly when touched (approximately 1 hour).
6. Remove cakes from oven. Cool 5 minutes, then turn
cakes out of pans and cool on wire racks. Serve
at room temperature with caramel sauce, whipped
cream, or fresh cherries.

"Um . . . I'm not very good at this," Sébastien said, opening
and closing cupboard doors, looking for a mixing bowl.

"Me neither," Olivia said. "But how hard can it be? We
just follow the recipe, right?"

"Right," Sébastien said uncertainly. "Does this look big
enough?" He held out an enormous ceramic bowl.

Olivia laughed. "I think we could make eight cakes in that
one, Seb."

They took turns reading out the directions. Olivia found
an eggbeater in a drawer and used it to beat the eggs with
the butter and sugar. She clanged the blades against the side
of the bowl, and a glob of batter sprayed up and spattered
her glasses. "Oops," she said, wiping the surface with her shirt
sleeve. Greasy streaks smudged the glass.

"Okay, that looks mixed enough," Sébastien said. "What's
next?"

Olivia peered at the recipe. "Four and a quarter cups of
sifted flour."

Sébastien found a sifter and dumped the flour in. As he
enthusiastically pulled the handle, a fine white cloud floated
up and coated the smudges on Olivia's glasses.

They measured out the spices, and Olivia added them to
the flour.

"Mmm, smells good," she said. "I bet it'll be delicious."

She held up the recipe. "Last ingredient. One and a half cups of baking soda."

Sébastien measured it and stirred it into the flour and spices. Then they mixed the wet and dry ingredients together, alternating with the buttermilk and finishing with the dry mixture, just like the recipe said. The batter was nice and bubbly, a beautiful rich shade of brown. Carefully, they poured it into the pans and slid it into the oven.

They surveyed the kitchen. Mounds of flour, globs of the sugar-butter-and-eggs mixture, puddles of buttermilk, and dustings of spice littered the counters, table, and floor.

"We're not exactly the neatest cooks," Olivia said with a laugh. She filled the sink with soapy water while Sébastien gathered up the dishes.

"Turn off the water for a sec," he said. "Do you hear something?"

Olivia listened. There was a faint popping sound coming from the oven. "Just the cake baking, I guess. Doesn't it smell good?"

Sébastien nodded. "Do you think we should check on it?"

She shook her head. "I heard Gen say that you shouldn't open the oven door too much while a cake is baking. Makes it go flat or something."

She continued filling the sink. Sébastien started wiping the counters.

The popping sound grew louder. They exchanged a look. "Maybe we'd better." Olivia said.

Sébastien carefully opened the oven door. The surfaces of the cakes were bubbling. Small burps rose to the top and burst, sending bits of batter shooting up to the oven ceiling, where they scorched with a hissing sound.

As Sébastien and Olivia watched in disbelief, the bubbles became larger. They exploded in larger bursts, with louder splats. Acrid smoke, smelling of burned sugar, started wafting out of the oven.

"Oh no," Sébastien said, overcome with growing horror, yet unable to do anything but stand there and watch.

"I think we'd better take –" Olivia began.

The largest burst yet arose from the middle of one pan. It shot up to the oven ceiling, dripped down onto the cake, and splatted onto the floor of the oven, where it instantly scorched, sending more smoke billowing out into the room.

The smoke alarm started buzzing, a piercing blast that shrilled over . . . and over . . . and over . . .

While Sébastien stood there, paralyzed, Olivia sprang into action. Running to fetch oven mitts, she carefully pulled out the pans and set them down in the sink. Along the way, more explosions burst over the edges and splatted onto the floor.

Grandma, Eve, Charlie, Geneviève, Alex, and Claire came running.

"Oh my God! Are you okay?"

"What did you do? Is there a fire?"

"What a mess!"

It took two hours to scour the oven, not to mention scrubbing the counters, floors, table, and sink.

When they had finished cleaning, Sébastien flopped into a chair. Olivia washed her face and her filthy glasses, then joined him at the table.

"I can't imagine what we did wrong," Sébastien said. "We

followed the recipe exactly, right?"

Olivia started laughing.

"What?" Sébastien asked.

Olivia could only shake her head and point to the recipe.

Sébastien looked. For the amount of baking soda, it said "one and a half teaspoons."

He started laughing too. "You mean we . . . one and a half *cups?* Oh my goodness."

They both roared.

"Kaboom!" Sébastien said.

FIFTEEN

PARTY-CRASHERS

"Let me guess," Geneviève said smugly, "by making the cake you discovered that Rachel and Chad were secretly planning to blow up the island."

"Very funny," Sébastien said, gritting his teeth.

"Rachel and Chad – bird-watching terrorists," Geneviève added.

"All right already," Sébastien began angrily, but Olivia chuckled. "It *was* hilarious," she admitted. "And it was all my fault. My glasses were so dirty, I read the recipe wrong."

"Yeah, I'd say putting in about twenty times too much baking soda was a little mistake," Geneviève said.

Everyone laughed.

"So . . ." Geneviève went on, "do you admit you were completely wrong about Rachel and Chad? Can we forget about them now?"

"No," Sébastien said.

Everyone looked at him in surprise.

"Just because Liv and I blew it with the cake doesn't mean that they aren't up to something. I still think they were a little too eager to get that recipe. We need to find out what they're up to."

"For crying out loud, Sébastien! Let it go," Geneviève said.

But he couldn't. So after Geneviève, Alex, and Claire left – having decided to look one more time for the door that fit the key – Sébastien and Olivia climbed on their bikes and started pedaling to Rachel and Chad's house.

"Today's Chad's birthday," he reminded her. "With a crowd around, we might be able to sneak in undetected and do a little sleuthing."

"You mean crash the party?" Olivia said, eyes wide behind her glasses.

"No!" Sébastien said. "They can't know we're there. I don't want to tip them off. We just want to look around and see if we can find anything suspicious."

"Like?"

"No idea," he admitted, riding along. "A note from Tantalus about the mine? Scribbles on the recipe they borrowed? Anything."

"I'm on the case, sir," Olivia said, giving a little salute, but then she stopped her bike short.

"What?" Sébastien said, braking to a stop beside her.

"Look at those violets," she said, pointing to a clump of flowers beside the road. "Did you ever see them in that shade before? What would you call that? Teal? Turquoise? Isn't it beautiful?"

"Liv!"

"Sorry, one minute." She hopped off her bike, picked a few of the blooms, and tucked them in her shorts pocket. "I've got to show these to Grandma."

By the time they dropped their bikes in the trees behind Rachel and Chad's, they could tell that the party was in full swing. Several cars were parked in the driveway, country and western music was blaring from the windows, and delicious smells were coming from the kitchen.

Sébastien looked left, right, then dashed to the back wall, Olivia on his heels. Hugging the house, they made their way around the back wall and then along the side. A deck, festooned with balloons and HAPPY BIRTHDAY banners, wrapped around the house from the side and continued around the front. Sébastien straightened up slowly and peeked over the deck floor, which was at the level of his chest. The kitchen was at the front of the house; standing on tiptoes, he could see the refrigerator through a side window. The kitchen seemed to be empty. Apparently the guests were all out on the deck on the other side of the house.

"This is our chance to look for the recipe and see if they've written anything on it," Sébastien whispered.

"Are you going in?"

"Not sure. Just want to peek through the window first."

"Me too!"

Hooking their feet on the deck floor and holding onto the wooden railing, they managed to pull themselves up onto the deck, then climbed up on the railing and flattened themselves against the side of the house. From the other end of the deck, a child's voice called over the music, "Look, Uncle Chad, I can balance a jellybean on my nose!" There was a peal of laughter.

Olivia, who was nearer the front of the house, carefully peeked around the corner. As they had suspected, all the guests were at the other end, where a picnic table and chairs had been set up. She nodded to Sébastien, and they inched their way sideways along the railing, moving closer to the kitchen window. Carefully they peered inside. All they could see was a mess of dishes, glasses, and serving trays strewn with the remains of cheese and crackers, veggies and dip, a broccoli casserole, and the skeleton of a large fish.

"See anything?" Sébastien whispered.

"There's a paper on the counter with writing on it, but I can't quite see it. Let me just –"

Twisting, Olivia leaned forward, craning her neck, trying to get a better view – and lost her balance. "Whoa . . ." Feeling herself falling forward, toward the house, she desperately thrust herself backward. "Whoa . . ." Arms windmilling, she found her balance, then kept tilting backward. "Whoa!" As she fell, Sébastien reached out to grab her, and he toppled backward too. They both landed on the grass beneath the deck.

Whumph!

"Ow!"

They scrambled to their feet, Olivia groping for her glasses in the grass and shoving them back on.

"What was that?" Rachel cried.

Chad was already running across the deck.

"Let's go!" Olivia hissed.

Sébastien started to get up. "Ow, my ankle!" He started hopping.

"What the – ?" Chad said, coming to a stop at the end of the deck.

Rachel caught up. "Who is it – oh! Hi."

"What are you doing here?" Chad said.

They stood at the railing, staring down at the two children.

Mute, Sébastien waited in dread. He and Olivia were in for it now. Chad and Rachel would not be amused that they were being spied on. They would demand an explanation. They would call Grandma. And when he and Liv got home, they would no doubt be severely punished. Sébastien envisioned spending the rest of his vacation in his room.

To his amazement, Olivia stepped forward, a smile on her face. "We brought you these," she said, and pulled the rather crushed violets from her pocket. "Grandma always garnished her *Brown Sugar Spice Cake* with violets. But it wasn't in her recipe, and she forgot to tell you. So we thought you would want to make the cake just the way Grandma did."

Picking up the thread, Sébastien nodded. "Yeah, that's right. But we didn't want to disturb the party. So we were just going to leave the flowers in the kitchen for you."

Rachel and Chad gaped. By this time, the rest of the guests had come up behind them, saying "What is it?" and "What's going on?" and "Who are they?"

"How sweet!" said Rachel, just as Chad said, "Are you okay? Did you fall off the deck or something?"

"It's nothing," Sébastien said. "We really should be going."

"That's so thoughtful of you," Rachel said.

"We should check you out, make sure you're not hurt," Chad said. "In fact, my brother-in-law is a paramedic. Howie, come here for a minute."

"No, no, we're fine," Olivia said quickly. She darted forward and handed the flowers to Rachel.

"Enjoy the *Brown Sugar Spice Cake!*" she said.

"And happy birthday, Chad!"

SIXTEEN

DON'T ATTACK AT DAWN

"So, did you two sleuths find out what those devils Rachel and Chad are up to?" Geneviève asked the next morning.

Olivia turned pink.

Sébastien scowled. "And did you three detectives find the lock that fit the key?"

That shut Geneviève up.

———

Grandma pulled out all her recipes. She lined up the key, the flashlight, the prism, the paintbrush, and the knitting needle on the counter, then called the grandchildren together. "We've got five clues," she reminded them. "Let's find some more!"

Claire found a recipe for *Cauliflower au gratin* on which Grandpa had written *Je t'aime, mon petit chou-fleur*. "Look!" she cried. "That must mean something."

Grandma only blushed.

Geneviève whispered, "It means, 'I love you, my little cabbage.'"

"Grandma!" Claire hooted. "Gross!"

Everyone laughed.

Suddenly Grandma stabbed her finger at a page. "Here's one!"

It was her recipe for *Zucchini Pickles*. Beneath the title was one of Grandpa's notations.

Zucchini Pickles

Magical liquid, magical brew,
Gives pickles their tang — and cleans windows too!

Ingredients:
2 pounds zucchini (5 or 6 medium), sliced 1/8-inch thick
2 medium onions, sliced thin
1/4 cup salt
2 cups apple cider vinegar
1 1/2 cups sugar
2 teaspoons yellow mustard seed
1 teaspoon celery seed

Instructions:
1. Slice zucchini and onions into a large ceramic bowl. Toss with salt, and cover with ice water. Let stand for 2 hours, then drain thoroughly.
2. Combine the remaining ingredients in a saucepan and bring to a boil. Simmer for 5 minutes.
3. Divide the zucchini and onions into 4 sterilized pint jars. Pour the liquid into each jar. Top with sterilized lids.
4. If you're going to eat them within a month, you can keep them in the fridge. If you want to keep them longer, process in a boiling-water bath for 10 minutes.

"*Magical liquid, magical brew*?" Olivia said. "What on earth is he talking about?"

Grandma smiled. "Vinegar, of course." She rummaged around in a cupboard and pulled out a bottle of apple cider vinegar. Wrapped around the neck was the familiar piece of fishing line. The tag said number 3.

"Grandma, you're brilliant!" Alex said, hugging her. "Can we make the pickles? Please?"

Grandma ruffled his hair. "I know how much you love pickles, Alex. I remember when you ate a whole jar of them all by yourself. But I don't think we should stop now. I promise that once we find the deed, we'll make a great big batch. How's that?"

Gazing longingly at the recipe, Alex sighed, then nodded.

———•———

That afternoon, while Grandma was napping, the cousins went to the beach. Sébastien's ankle hurt, so he stayed behind. He decided to tackle Ted's slip of paper again. Maybe, he thought, limping upstairs to Grandpa's desk, he'd see it with fresh eyes and the solution would leap out at him.

It didn't. He couldn't make any sense of the bold and plain letters, although he was still convinced that there was some kind of secret pattern to them.

That gave him an idea. He turned on Grandpa's computer and typed SECRET CODES into the search engine. This led to a series of Web pages describing all kinds of encoding techniques.

First he read about the Winding Road Cipher, where you wrote the real message in a horizontal grid and then wrote the fake message using another pattern. So if your message was ATTACK AT DAWN, you created the secret code by writing:

ATTA

CKAT

DAWN

Then, reading vertically, you presented the fake message as: ACD TKA TAW ATN.

Or, reading in a counter-clockwise spiral from the top left: ACD AWN TAT TKA.

Which was fun, but there was nothing like that on the slip.

Seb clicked on another secret code called the Rail Fence Cipher. With this code, you wrote your message on alternating lines:

A　　T　　C　　A　　D　　W

　　T　　A　　K　　T　　A　　N

Then, reading across, you combined letters to make an unreadable message: ATCADW TAKTAN.

Maybe, Seb thought excitedly, that's what the writer of the slip of paper had done with the bold letters. He copied them on alternating lines:

t　a　m　i　e　t　b　e　f　e　t　s...

　I　d　m　g　I　w　g　a　e　o　l　　e...

Then, reading across, he tried to put them together into words. But what on earth could **tamietbefets** or **IdmgIwgaeole** mean? Nothing!

Sébastien slammed his hand on the desk. He was wasting time, going down dead ends, and meanwhile, Tantalus Mining was moving ahead with its plans to take over Grandma's property. He *had* to figure this out.

He couldn't.

He stabbed the power button and the screen went blank.

SEVENTEEN

A LITTLE PRIVATE CELEBRATION

The next day, Sébastien and Olivia rode their bikes to the general store, Sébastien to get coffee beans for his mom, Olivia to get paint thinner for Grandma. When they approached the cash register, they saw that Chad and Rachel were at the counter, unloading a basket full of items. Embarrassed, Seb and Olivia ducked behind the fish counter.

"Look at all these goodies," Muriel said cheerfully. "Baguette and brie, sparkling grape juice, cherries, pâté, chocolate – wow! What's the occasion?"

"We're going on a picnic," Chad informed her. "A little private celebration."

"Oh?" Muriel said in that curious voice. "Good news?"

"Mmm-hmm," Chad said, but he didn't volunteer anything more.

Muriel continued ringing up the purchases. "Going anyplace special?"

"To the top of Lookout Hill Road," Rachel said.

"Right where they're putting the mine?" Muriel said, sounding aghast. "Why there, of all places?"

Sébastien elbowed Olivia. She returned an alarmed look.

"It has such a beautiful view," Rachel said.

"That it does," Muriel sighed. "I just hope it stays that way."

After they paid for their own purchases, Sébastien and Olivia hurried out to confer.

"I *knew* they were up to something," Sébastien said.

"Probably celebrating selling their land to Tantalus. Why else would they have all that money to spend? Before, they said they were broke."

"Or maybe —" Sébastien's eyes grew wide, "they *did* figure out something from the recipe. Maybe they've found Grandma's deed."

"And are getting a big payoff from Tantalus."

"There's only one thing to do," Sébastien said.

———•———

"Not this again!" Geneviève yelled when Olivia and Sébastien told the others what they had heard.

Alex shook his head. "I don't know, Gen. There could be something to it. Why else would they have money all of a sudden?"

"They won the lottery," Geneviève said, rolling her eyes. "They inherited a fortune from dear old Aunt Agatha. How should I know?"

"I like Rachel and Chad," Claire said in a troubled voice. "I wish they weren't up to something bad."

"For crying out loud, not you too, Claire," Geneviève said, exasperated. "You're all nuts. And I'm not spying on their picnic like some demented private eye!"

"Then don't come," Sébastien said. "We'll go without you."

Of course that did it. There was no way Geneviève was going to be left out. An hour later, she was in the line of bikes pedaling up Lookout Hill Road. Leading steadily upward, the road wound in a slow spiral around the hill, offering views, first to the east and the village, then to the north and Seal Bay, then to the west, past Hugh's Perch to Heron Island, and finally to the south, overlooking Grandma's, Muriel's, and Osprey Cove.

Huffing, furious that she'd been corralled into this ridiculous outing, and even more furious that they would have gone without her, Geneviève stopped to catch her breath. In the pit of her stomach was an uncomfortable thought: what if Sébastien was right? The whole theory that Rachel and Chad were trying to steal Grandma's deed was crazy, she knew that. And yet Sébastien was so darn smart. He knew all kinds of things, had a memory like a trap, and had gotten lots of practice with Grandpa at solving mysteries. What if he was on to something?

Standing on her pedals, she rode hard, trying to catch up to the others. No, she decided, it just wasn't possible. Sébastien was just getting carried away with all his suspicions. Rachel and Chad. Charlie. Shane.

Her heart gave a little leap at the thought of Shane, of the kisses they'd shared. Recently, they'd met by the public beach and hid in some reeds to make out. Strange, she thought, that Shane had been to her place several times but she had never been to his. In fact, she still had no idea where he and his mom lived. All he'd said was that it was a cabin and that he and Geneviève would have no privacy there.

Well, no matter. Last time, he'd taken her out to teach her how to surf. And even though she hadn't been very good at it, falling off her board more than she managed to stay on it, she hadn't minded one bit. Each time she fell off, Shane swam up to her, put his hands on her waist, and lifted her back up.

—•

Just before the crest of the hill, Sébastien motioned for them to stop pedaling. They wiped their sweaty faces and gulped from their water bottles. Moving onto the grass to muffle their footsteps, they walked their bikes to the top of the hill and laid them down behind a stand of caragana bushes. Bees flew in and out of the yellow blooms.

Peeking over the top of the bushes, Sébastien could see Rachel and Chad stretched out on a brown-and-green woven blanket, leaning on their elbows facing one another. Between them was a picnic basket, with an array of plates, bowls, and glasses spread out on the blanket.

Smells of ripe cheese and spicy-sweet cherries floated on the air.

"I'm hungry," Claire whispered.

"Sh!" Sébastien hissed.

Rachel tore off a hunk of bread, placed a wedge of cheese on top of it, and took a bite. "Mmm . . . isn't this brie delicious?"

"Sure is," Chad said. He ate the slice of bread and cheese, then licked his fingers.

"Cherries?"

"Thanks." Rachel took a handful.

For a while, the only noise was the sound of pits hitting a bowl. Then Chad said, "Say, where's that chocolate? We'd better eat it before it melts."

Rachel rooted around in the picnic basket. "Oh, it *is* soft." She peeled back the wrapping. Geneviève could see that the chocolate had bent over from the heat. Laughing, Rachel tried to break off a piece, but it smooshed all over her fingers.

"Here," she said, holding out her hand.

Chad leaned forward and started licking the chocolate off Rachel's fingers.

"That tickles," she said with a giggle.

Chad worked his way from Rachel's fingers, across her palm, to her wrist.

"Hey!" Rachel said. Then, "Mmm . . ." Then, "*Mmmm . . .*" The next moment she had tossed the chocolate back into the picnic basket and was leaning forward and kissing Chad on the lips.

Claire stuck out her tongue as if she was going to throw up. Alex and Olivia covered their eyes. Sébastien grimaced. Only Geneviève didn't seem to mind – although she did turn pink.

Thankfully, at that moment a chipmunk darted across the picnic blanket, its tail brushing Rachel's leg.

"Oh!" she exclaimed, sitting up. "What was that?"

Chad pointed. "That little rascal."

They both laughed and Chad lifted a bottle. "Here, let me refill your glass." He poured a fizzy purple liquid into Rachel's glass, then filled his own and raised it in the air. "A toast."

"To our future."

"Our prosperous future."

They clinked glasses and drank.

Yeah, stolen from Grandma, Sébastien thought. He exchanged a look with the others.

"Just as soon as we sign the agreement tomorrow," Rachel said. "You don't think anything could go wrong, do you?"

Chad shook his head. "He said it was a done deal. No need to keep it a secret once the paperwork is done."

The paperwork, Sébastien thought. Did that mean the sale of their house – or the transfer of the deed?

"If things go well, we'll move to the other side of the island," Rachel said. "It's nicer over there. We'll have a view like that." She pointed toward the southwest – *in the direction of Grandma's place.*

"Imagine. Our own little windfall," Chad said. "Whoever would have thought we could pull it off?"

Sébastien could stand it no longer. He strode out from behind the caragana bushes and pointed at them. "How could you?"

Rachel gasped.

Chad jerked and spilled his juice. "What are you doing here? Once was a bit much, but this is getting ridiculous!"

"Why are you following us?" asked Rachel.

"How could we *what?*" Chad said, looking baffled.

"Steal our Grandma's deed."

"What!"

The others came out to join Sébastien.

"You figured it out from the recipe, didn't you?" Olivia said.

"The recipe? What recipe?" Rachel said.

"*Brown Sugar Spice Cake,*" said Claire.

"Huh?"

"Don't pretend," Sébastien said. "We know why you borrowed it."

"To make it for Chad's birthday?" Rachel said, sounding bewildered.

"No! To figure out where the deed was," Alex said.

"You kids are crazy!" Chad shouted.

Rachel said, "I think you'd better tell us what you're talking about."

Angrily, Sébastien laid out the case. When he finished, there was a short silence before Chad burst out laughing. But Rachel did not seem amused. She put her hands on her hips. "How could you think we'd do such a thing?"

For the first time, Sébastien began to get a very uncomfortable feeling.

"Then what were you celebrating?" he asked in a much quieter voice.

"We got the permit to start our bird-watching business!"

"It's our dream come true," Chad said. "Now we won't have to leave the island."

"Then . . . you don't know anything about Grandma's deed?" Olivia said in a small voice.

"Of course not!" Rachel said.

"Only that we hope she finds it," Chad added.

"And . . . you're not selling your place to Tantalus?" Alex asked.

"Never!"

"But you said . . . we heard you say that you might," Sébastien said feebly.

"Only as a last resort," Rachel said. "But even then, we couldn't bring ourselves to do it."

"Can you imagine the effect the mine is going to have on the birds?" Chad said angrily. "How could we support that?"

Rachel threw her head back and burst out laughing. "You crazy kids! So that's why you've been spying on us."

"Well . . . ," Sébastien said with a sheepish smile, "we

thought . . ."

"*I* didn't," Geneviève announced. She gave Rachel a conspiratorial look. "I never believed that stuff for a minute. I kept telling them they were deluded, the poor children."

"We were only trying to protect Grandma," Olivia said.

"And boy, did you do a good job," Chad said, laughing, "even if you were totally off base."

Sébastien, Alex, Claire, and Olivia stood there, red-faced.

Rachel held out her arms. "Come on. I think you all need some chocolate."

<hr />

Five minutes later, the cousins were delightfully filled up with bread, cheese, cherries, and melted chocolate. Claire, Alex, and Olivia were telling them about the quest to find Grandma's deed.

Geneviève leaned close to Sébastien. "I told you."

"You don't have to rub it in," Sébastien said gloomily. "Besides, just because I was wrong this time doesn't mean I'm wrong all the time."

"Like with Shane," Geneviève said heatedly. "The poor guy makes a mistake about the bioluminescence, and do you give him the benefit of the doubt? No. In your world, he's plotting against us. Give it up, Seb!"

At Geneviève's raised voice, Rachel turned from her conversation with the others. "Give what up, Gen?"

"Sébastien and his paranoid theories," she answered. "He suspects everybody, not just you two. You know Shane, the surfer guy?"

When Rachel nodded, Geneviève went on, "My brilliant

brother has this crazy idea that Shane is also trying to keep us from finding the deed."

Sébastien squirmed.

"Well," Rachel said, "it wouldn't be much of a stretch, considering his connections."

"What do you mean?" Geneviève asked.

"His uncle?"

"Huh?"

Rachel looked at her. "Didn't you know that Shane was Stan Wilensky's nephew?"

"What?" Geneviève felt her cheeks flame.

"What!" Sébastien said.

"His mom is Wilensky's sister," Chad said. "You didn't know?"

For a moment, Geneviève couldn't speak. "No . . . I . . ."

"Wilensky got his sister a job with Tantalus – that's why they moved here, apparently," Chad said.

"They're staying in the cottage on Wilensky's land for now, but I hear they're looking for a permanent home," Rachel put in.

Geneviève felt all the heat drain from her face. A cold sweat broke out on her forehead. *Shane, Wilensky's nephew!*

Why hadn't he told her? Had he purposely kept it from her? Was that why he hadn't shown her where he and his mom were living – because he didn't want her to know about the connection?

What did it mean? Did it mean anything? Geneviève took a deep breath.

No, she decided. Shane wouldn't have had any reason to keep his relation to Wilensky a secret. It just hadn't come up.

After all, she'd never asked him if he had any relatives on the island. And maybe he was embarrassed that he and his mom were living in a small cottage that belonged to a wealthier relation, and that was why he'd never taken her there.

Geneviève heaved a sigh. That must be it.

She managed a smile and a careless wave of the hand. "No big deal."

Within minutes, she'd corralled the rest of them and they were getting back on their bikes to head home.

—●—

Sébastien waited for Alex, Claire, and Olivia to take off. He pulled Geneviève aside. But before he could open his mouth, she jerked her arm away. "Don't say a word!"

"But Gen —"

"It's none of your business."

"But don't you think it's suspicious —"

"It doesn't mean a thing."

"What, that he never told you?"

"It never came up, that's all. I'm not in the habit of asking guys who they're related to. Which you wouldn't know because you don't date yet."

"Gen —"

"I don't want to hear it. It doesn't change anything. He's a good guy." She hopped onto her pedals. "So shut up about it!" She sped away down the hill.

EIGHTEEN

ALPHABET + THREE = NOTHING

The next morning, Geneviève was lounging on the deck with Sébastien and Claire, watching her mom and Charlie, who were strolling at the water's edge. As a wave rolled in, Eve stomped on the water with her bare foot, splashing Charlie. He roared, chasing her as she ran out of reach. When the next wave rolled in, Charlie splashed her back, and Geneviève could see the dark patch where her rolled-up pants were wet.

"Got you!" she heard, followed by Charlie's booming laugh.

Eve skittered away, her laughter floating over the sound of the waves. When Charlie caught up to her, he pulled her close. She lifted her face and they kissed.

Geneviève smiled, remembering her own kisses. It was fun to be in love – and, if her mom was any indication, it didn't matter whether you were young or old. It was still a thrill. Sure, Geneviève thought, she'd had an uncomfortable moment when she'd found out that Shane was Wilensky's nephew. But he'd just texted her and asked her to meet him for another surfing lesson. She knew what that meant.

The phone rang, and she ran inside to answer it.

"Is Charlie McNulty there?" a man's voice asked.

"Uh . . . not at the moment," Geneviève said. "Can I take a message?"

"Sure. Tell him Stan Wilensky called. It's about the matter we discussed."

She stood there, silent.

"Did you get that?"

"Uh . . . yeah, I'll tell him. What's the number?"

"He has it."

Dazed, Geneviève hung up and stumbled outside.

"Who was it?" Claire asked.

Gen hesitated. "Stan Wilensky," she said. "For Charlie." She repeated what Wilensky had said.

"See!" Sébastien said. "Now do you believe me?"

Geneviève felt her heart sink. She hadn't believed it, had refused to believe it, but how could she go on denying what was right in front of her? "Well . . ."

Claire shook her head. "Look at him," she said. They all looked out toward the beach again. Eve and Charlie were sitting on a boulder, their legs dangling over the edge. Charlie leaned close and whispered something in Eve's ear, and she reached up and stroked his cheek. "He's so sweet. How could he be plotting to hurt Mom and Grandma?"

"Claire!" Sébastien said. "He's taking calls from Stan Wilensky!"

"I know, but –"

"Look, I was wrong about Rachel and Chad. I admit it. But with Charlie, it's clear-cut. We've caught him plotting with the enemy."

Geneviève sighed. "It does look bad."

"It doesn't *look* bad, it *is* bad!" Sébastien said. "And we've got to tell Mom – now, before he gets away with it."

Geneviève sighed. After all those happy thoughts about

love . . ."I suppose you're right. Oh, poor Mom! She's going to be so heartbroken –"

"No!" Claire yelled. "I – I know it looks bad, but I just don't believe Charlie would –"

"But Claire –"

"No!"

"Shush!" Geneviève said. "They're coming."

The three children waited silently as Eve and Charlie climbed the steps from the beach to the deck. Their hair was windblown, and they were grinning broadly.

Brushing sand from her feet, Eve said, "You're awfully quiet. Is everything okay?"

"Everything's just fine," Geneviève said in a hearty voice. "Oh, Charlie, you got a phone call. From Stan Wilensky."

Eve jerked her head. "Stan Wilensky?"

Charlie turned red. "Yeah . . . I was, uh, asking about getting a seat on the float plane tomorrow. Got to go back and straighten things out at the office."

"You never told me!"

"Just for the day. I'll be back by evening." Edging toward the house, he said, "I'd, uh, better call him back."

He went inside.

Eve looked after him with an odd expression.

Geneviève looked away.

——●——

Charlie's betrayal made Sébastien even more determined to figure out what was going on with that slip of paper from Ted. He went up to Grandpa's office and turned on the computer. Once again, he typed SECRET CODES into the search engine and, after several clicks, came to a page titled Caesar's Cipher. This secret code, he read, had reportedly been used by Julius Caesar to plan secret attacks. And it was pretty simple to use: You just chose a number and replaced each letter in the written text with the letter that number of places further along in the alphabet. So, for example, if you had the word APPLE and the number was five, by moving each letter five places along, APPLE turned into FTTQJ.

Which, Sébastien thought, was a nonsense word – but Caesar's Cipher still might have been the method used to disguise the words on the slip of paper.

Excitedly he referred to the list he'd written down earlier of the letters written in bold:

t I a d m m i g e I t w b g e a f e e o t l s e h e d h i t n m i r j e t p r i s i p t s h p e f b i s w d

But what number had they used for the cipher? Sébastien scanned the slip, looking for clues. The only bit that had anything to do with numbers was "fish, birds, and wildlife." Three things. Not much to go on, but maybe the key number was three.

Beneath the row of letters, he wrote the letter three places on.

W l d g p p l j h l w e j...
Gobbledygook!
But maybe he was supposed to use the plain letters.
W k h r w h u v o q w d q w d o x l...
More gobbledygook. He threw down his pencil in disgust. Back to the computer.

On another site he discovered the Vigenère Cipher. This was much more complicated – and much more sophisticated.

First, Sébastien found, you had to set up a table where you wrote out the alphabet twenty-six times, each row beginning with the next letter of the alphabet. So:

A   B   C   D   E ...
B   C   D   E   F ...
C   D   E   F   G ...
D   E   F   G   H ... and so on.

Then you chose a keyword with the same number of letters as the word you wanted to hide. So, if your code word was OTTER, the keyword had to have five letters also – say, CLOWN.

Then you had to create the cipher – the fake word that hid the code word. To do this, you took the first letter of the keyword, C, went to the row in the table beginning with C, found out what letter was in column O – in this case, Q – and wrote that down.

Then you went to row L and wrote down the letter in column T, which was E.

So, using the keyword CLOWN, the cipher for OTTER was QEHAE.

Going in reverse, you used the keyword and the alphabet table to decode the cipher and arrive back at the secret word.

Sébastien's excitement grew as he copied out the table and figured out how to convert OTTER into QEHAE and back again. Grandpa would've loved this, he thought, running his finger across the rows and columns to find the hidden letters.

Eagerly, he chose the first letter in the list of bold letters – and then stopped short. There was one big flaw in his system. To use the Vigenère Cipher, the person who created the secret message had to pass on the keyword to the person who was supposed to unscramble it.

Sébastien didn't know the keyword. Without it, there was no way he could figure out how to decode the letters. He had the first letter, T, but no idea where to look on the table. If he looked in row T, column A, he got T. If he looked in row T, column B, he got U. There were twenty-four more possibilities.

Sébastien pounded his hand on the table. This was hopeless. He was floundering around with secret codes and theories and puzzles, and he was getting nowhere. And meanwhile, Charlie was plotting with Wilensky and Saxby to help the mine go through.

Oh, if only Grandpa were here, Sébastien thought, dropping his chin on his hands. He'd figure out the darn message and stop Charlie in his tracks.

But then, if Grandpa were here, the cottage wouldn't be threatened in the first place.

With a strangled laugh at his own tortured logic, he turned off the computer.

NINETEEN

"YOU'VE GOT ONE WEEK"

G randma and the children were back at the kitchen table, going through the recipes. Alex had just found a notation in the recipe for *Caraway Rye Bread* that said "*So delish I'm caraawayed!*" – and had gotten all excited, until Grandma explained that Grandpa was just making a joke out of caraway and carried away – when there was a knock at the front door.

"I'll get it," said Claire, running to open it.

There stood Mark Saxby, Valerie London, and Wayne Cheng.

Mark Saxby said, "Aren't you the little girl who was choking the other day?"

"Yes."

"Are you all right now?"

"Yes, thank you."

"Excellent." Smiling, he patted Claire on the head. "Is your grandmother home?"

"I'll get her," Claire said. She ran back to the kitchen. Grandma and the children were laughing, pointing at something in one of the cookbooks.

"Grandma?" Claire said.

"Yes, sweetheart?" Grandma said, still chuckling as she looked up.

"The Tantalus Mining people are here."

A hush fell over the table. Grandma went pale. "Oh, dear. I – oh, dear." She swallowed. "Could you show them into the living room? I'll be right in."

"I'll get Mom," Sébastien said. "And Charlie," he added, though he wasn't sure that was a good idea. Still, better to keep Charlie where they could see him than to let him hide in the background.

By the time Sébastien came downstairs with Eve and Charlie, the children and the Tantalus people were in the living room. Saxby, London, and Cheng were squished on the couch, looking uncomfortable and hot in their city clothes. The cousins were sitting across from them, on the floor.

Grandma came in, and Mark Saxby stood up. Or, he tried to. First he had to unwedge himself from the other two, who nearly toppled over when he removed his body from the couch. They shot to their feet too.

"Good afternoon, Mrs. Honeyman. So good to see you," Saxby said.

Grandma didn't return the greeting, though she did nod and make introductions: "My daughter, Eve Brossard, and her friend, Charles McNulty."

Sébastien watched closely. A look passed between Charlie and Mark Saxby, though neither man said anything to indicate that they'd already met.

You lying weasel, Sébastien thought. No matter that Charlie actually had flown to the mainland and back the day before, just like he'd said. That didn't mean he wasn't lying about everything else.

The three company representatives wedged themselves

back onto the couch.

"Well, Mrs. Honeyman," Mark Saxby said with a smile, "I wonder if you've had a chance to reconsider our very generous offer." He opened his briefcase, withdrew a sheaf of papers, and placed them on the coffee table.

Grandma shook her head. "I told you before, Mr. Saxby, that I have no interest in selling."

Saxby's smile twitched. "Now, listen here –" he began.

Valerie London put her hand on his arm. She turned to Grandma, and the thick gold links of her necklace flashed. "Mrs. Honeyman," she said sweetly, "I'm not sure you understand just how impressive this offer is. We are prepared to pay well above the market price. Why, you'd be able to relocate anywhere you liked, from one of the other islands to a penthouse in downtown Vancouver!"

Grandma opened her mouth, but Eve spoke first. "I don't think *you* understand, Ms. London. This is my mother's home. She is not going to sell it – for any price."

Valerie London's face flushed.

"I was afraid you were going to stick to that regrettable position," Mark Saxby said. "Very well, Mrs. Honeyman. We expect to get the permit in three days. At that point, if you have not accepted our offer, you will be required to prove ownership of your property. As you know, if you cannot, your property will revert to the government, who no doubt will turn it over to us. If you do prove ownership, you can stay here. But I'm warning you that construction of the road to the mine will begin immediately, and the road will go right around your property. That may not be pleasant for you."

Grandma gasped.

"Are you threatening my mother?" Eve said.

"Of course not," Saxby said. "Simply stating the facts. The mine will soon be a reality –"

"If you get the permit," Eve said.

Saxby's face colored. "We are quite confident of that. After all, we made a very persuasive case for the project, showing significant economic and environmental benefits." He put the papers back in his briefcase. "I'm sorry it's come to this, Mrs. Honeyman. You can sell – or you can live next to the access road. It's your choice."

He wiggled forward on the couch to free himself and stand up. Valerie London and Wayne Cheng rose as well, straightening their clothes.

"If you change your mind, you know how to contact me," Mark Saxby said. "Good day."

He left, followed by London and Cheng.

Grandma put her face in her hands. "What am I going to do?"

"They're not going to get your home, Mom," Eve said.

"But what then?" Grandma lifted her head. "You heard him. Even if I find the deed, I still have the road on top of me. And if I can't produce the deed, the government will take my land–" She began to cry, the same heart-rending cries that Claire had heard the first day they'd come.

"But Grandma, we'll find the deed. We already have six clues. We must be close," Alex said.

Grandma shook her head. "It's no use. I thought maybe – but it's hopeless. The cottage is doomed." She burst into fresh sobs. Weeping, leaning on Eve and Charlie, she trudged upstairs. A moment later, the cousins heard the creak of her bed.

They looked at one another. No one said anything.
But all of them were thinking, *Three days.*
And now they had to do it without Grandma.

TWENTY

TREASURE IN THE SAND

The five cousins trooped back to the kitchen. They placed the key, the flashlight, the prism, the knitting needle, the vinegar, and the paintbrush in the middle of the table.

"Six things that have nothing to do with each other," Geneviève said. "What on earth are we supposed to do with them?"

"Well . . ." Alex began, "maybe the prism is supposed to hang from the knitting needle . . ."

"Or maybe the flashlight lights up the prism," Olivia said.

"Which focuses light on the vinegar and heats it up," Sébastien finished.

"That doesn't make any sense," Geneviève said.

"Well, I don't know!" Sébastien said.

"We're nowhere," Olivia said gloomily.

"No, we're not," Sébastien said. "At some point, Grandpa'll probably give us a clue that tells us what we're supposed to do with everything."

"But when?" Geneviève said. "We only have three days."

"I know that!" Sébastien said.

"If we hadn't wasted time spying on Rachel and Chad –"

"If we hadn't wasted time looking for bioluminescence –"

"Guys!" Alex shouted.

They all looked at him.

"We can't fight. We don't have time. We just have to keep going. Now, what is it about these six things that Grandpa wanted us to see?"

There was no answer.

"Okay," Alex said, "let's try it another way. Each one came from a clue in a recipe. So what is it about the recipes?"

Sébastien pointed to the knitting needle. "Well, the clue to that was in *Muriel's Berry Pandowdy.* And the only thing I know about that recipe is that it's my favorite."

Olivia pointed to the paintbrush. "*Painterman Eggs* is my favorite. All that gooey, runny yolk!"

"The flashlight came from *Emergency Fudge,*" Claire began, "and that's my all-time favorite candy, even if I did get a little sick –"

"Guys!" Alex interrupted. "Don't you see?"

"No. What?" Olivia said.

"Yes!" Geneviève said excitedly. "That's what Grandpa was doing! Putting the clues into our favorites – so we would find them!"

"Right!" Sébastien said. "So what do we have?" He started pointing to objects, then to people. "*Muriel's Berry Pandowdy* – me. *Painterman Eggs* – Liv. *Emergency Fudge* – Claire."

"*Sparkle Cookies* – Gen," Alex went on. "*Zucchini Pickles* – me. Who am I forgetting?"

"Oh, I get it," Olivia said. "*Pesto* – Grandma."

"Right, that was the first one," Alex said. "But there's got to be another clue, to tie them all together. Clue number 1. Who are we missing?"

"Grandpa!" Claire shouted.

"Of course," Sébastien said. "What was his favorite recipe?"

"*Osprey Cove Clam Pot!*" Alex and Claire said together.

Everyone started frantically paging through the recipes. Alex found it in the battered black notebook.

Osprey Cove Clam Pot
Treasure in the sand, treasure in the pot

Ingredients:
1 tablespoon olive oil
1 white onion
2 cloves garlic
1 1/2 pounds new potatoes
1 1/2 cups white wine or vegetable stock
1/2 teaspoon salt
1/4 teaspoon pepper
4 pounds fresh clams, cleaned
1 lemon

Instructions:
1. Clean clams according to instructions below.
2. Thinly slice onion; finely chop garlic. Halve potatoes and set aside.
3. Heat olive oil in a large pot over high heat. Add sliced onion and stir until it starts to brown, 6 to 8 minutes.
4. Add garlic and cook for 1 to 2 minutes until it starts to release a great smell. Add potatoes, wine or stock, and salt and pepper, and bring to a boil.

5. Cover the pot with a tight-fitting lid, reduce heat and simmer until potatoes are just barely tender, about 20 minutes.

6. Add clams and toss to distribute them throughout the pot. Cover and cook, shaking pot occasionally, until clams open (about 12 to 15 minutes).

7. Remember to discard any clams with unopened shells!

8. Cut lemon into quarters and arrange on plates.

9. Serve Clam Pot with crusty bread for soaking up the juices from the pot. Be sure to set bowls on the table for clam shells.

NOTE: The morning of the Clam Pot, dig fresh clams, being sure to toss back any that are too small. Cover clams with a damp cloth and place in the fridge.

Grandma's clam-cleaning tips:

1. Use clams within 24 hours of digging.

2. To clean clams, soak them in a bowl of cold water for 20 minutes. This will allow them to breathe and release any sand trapped in their shells.

3. Scrub each clam by hand before cooking to remove barnacles and seaweed from the shell.

4. Test that your clams are alive by tapping each one on the counter. If a clam's shell doesn't close, discard it.

Armed with sand shovels, the cousins hopped on their bikes and set off along the south shore for Osprey Cove. The road curved around a bend – and suddenly it ended, blocked off by a chain-link fence. The fence was six feet high, and it stretched away from either side of the road.

They braked to a stop.

"What the –" Claire began.

"Look," Sébastien said. He pointed to a sign hanging on the fence that read TANTALUS MINING ACCESS AREA – KEEP OUT.

"They can't do that!" Claire said. "They can't fence off Osprey Cove!"

But they had. The cousins stood there, straddling their bikes, staring up at the fence.

Alex looked at the others. "Are we going to let a stupid fence stop us?"

"No way!" Geneviève said. Hiding her bike in the grass, she bent down beside the fence, forming a platform with her hands. "Who's first?"

They walked the rest of the way to Osprey Cove, where the shoreline scooped out a natural bay. Flanking the cove on either side stood two ancient, dead cedar trees, on whose broken-off tops ospreys built their messy looking twig-and-bark nests every year.

Even as they watched, one of the white-and-brown-flecked birds floated over the cove, lazily circling down, down, down, until, with a sudden movement, it plunged into the water and emerged with a wiggling fish in its talons.

"Grandpa loved those birds," Olivia said, watching the osprey return to the nest with one flap of its great wings.

"Okay, the clue is *Treasure in the sand, treasure in the pot*," Geneviève said. "What did Grandpa want us to find?"

"Clams, I guess," Alex said.

Sébastien shook his head. "It must be something else. Something we can use."

They looked around. There were rocks, hunks of driftwood, tangles of seaweed, broken mussel shells. Nothing looked like a clue.

"Think," Olivia said. "Something in the sand. A treasure."

Alex and Claire turned toward each other, mouths open, eyes alight.

"What?" Olivia said.

"Pirate Harry's Pit," Alex said, grinning at Claire.

"What's Pirate Harry's Pit?" Geneviève asked.

"It's this funny little cave, under the bank," Alex said, heading toward the grass that ringed the beach. "Even at high tide, the water doesn't reach it, so the bottom stays dry."

"It's just about big enough for a kid to squeeze into," Claire added, trotting to catch up to him, the others following.

"When we were little, fishing here with Grandpa, he used to tell us stories about this character called Pirate Harry," Alex told them. "He had lost an eye in a duel with Scurvy Steve, and he commanded a ship with black sails."

"And he plundered the high seas," Claire said.

"And he hid treasure in the pit," Alex said.

"How come we don't know about Pirate Harry?" Olivia asked.

"'Cause you never went fishing with us," Alex said. "Grandpa made up the stories while we were waiting for a bite."

"We used to go into Pirate Harry's Pit and dig and dig and never find anything," Claire said, laughing. "And when we told Grandpa he was making it up, he said, 'Oh, Pirate Harry must have come back yesterday and dug his treasure up.'"

"There's this little stone shelf at the back, where we used to put seashells and pretend they were Pirate Harry's gold coins, remember, Claire?" Alex said.

She laughed in reply.

By now the cousins had reached the bank, which rose a couple of feet above the sandy beach. Claire and Alex started pushing aside the beach grass that hung down over the bank.

"What are we looking for?" Sébastien said.

"There's a kind of rocky ledge that juts out at the top," Claire said, "and the hole slants down, under the – Oh, Alex! I think I've got it!"

Everyone rushed over. Claire pushed back a clump of tan grass heads, and there was a shelf of slate, about four feet wide, that stuck out from under the thatch of grass. An oval-shaped hole, maybe three feet across, gaped beneath it.

"That's it, Claire!" Alex shouted. He began to scoop sand away from the lower lip of the hole, enlarging the entrance. Then he flung himself onto his stomach and reached into the hole.

"Anything?" Geneviève asked excitedly.

"No, just sand," Alex said. He squirmed to thrust his arm in at another angle, pushing his shoulder against the gap. "I can just feel the edge of that shelf at the back . . . but I can't get any farther."

He drew his arm out, looking disappointed.

Sébastien squatted and peered into the hole. "Claire, do you think you could still get in there?"

Claire knelt beside him. "I don't know. I was pretty small the last time." She stuck her head in. "Well . . . maybe. It's worth a try."

She flopped down on her stomach.

"Wait," Geneviève said. "Is it safe?"

Claire twisted around to look at her. "The top can't collapse, if that's what you mean. The worst that can happen is that I'll get stuck."

"Like Winnie-the-Pooh," Olivia said.

"Promise me you won't leave me here to get thin – or hang washing on my feet," Claire said with a laugh. She turned back to the hole and slithered forward so that her head and one shoulder were in, then twisted and slid her other shoulder inside. Her chest, then her hips, disappeared. Her legs twisted and turned; she flipped onto her side and drew one leg into the hole.

"Are you okay?" Geneviève called anxiously.

"Fine" came the muffled reply, from farther away. Then, "I'm at the shelf." More twisting. "Wait!" Very muffled. "I've got something!" She kicked her free foot. "Help me out!"

Carefully the cousins pulled, first one leg, then both, helping Claire slide backward, freeing her hips, her waist, her chest . . .

She twisted, pulling her shoulders out of the hole, then her head, covered in sand. She scrambled to her feet and held out –

– a miniature treasure chest.

It was made of metal. It had no decoration, no writing, on it. The top curved like a dome and its lip curled over the lower part, keeping dirt and moisture out. Aside from moss growing on top, and sand clinging to the bottom, it looked perfectly intact and in good shape.

"Oh my goodness!" Geneviève said.

"However did Grandpa get it in there?" Olivia said.

"Open it, open it!" Sébastien said.

Claire pushed upward on the lid with her thumbs. It didn't budge. She banged the handle of her sand shovel against the lip of the dome, tapping all around its underside. The dome sprang free.

Everyone crowded around. Inside was the usual nest of plastic boxes inside plastic boxes, each sealed with tape. Wrapped around the smallest box was a length of fishing line, with a tag that said number 1. Inside the box were two sheets of paper, folded up inside a plastic bag.

Claire drew out one sheet. It was thick and sturdy, like parchment. At the top it said MAP, but the rest was blank.

"Huh?" Alex said. "That's no use."

"Open the other one," Sébastien said.

Claire unfolded the second sheet. As she scanned it, her cheeks grew pink. "Oh, my," she said.

"What? *What?*" Geneviève asked.

Claire read aloud, "*My dearest Lily, if you have reached this letter, you have found the last clue —*"

"Hooray!" Alex shouted.

"Shush, Alex," Olivia scolded. "Go on, Claire."

"Oh, I'm so excited, I can hardly read," Claire said, but she continued, "*Use the objects in the order of the numbered tags to discover the deed. Good luck! I love you with all my heart. Sam*"

"We've got it!" Alex yelled. "Come on, let's go!"

TWENTY-ONE

"I REMEMBER!"

"We found it, we found it!" Sébastien yelled, running into the living room. There was no answer.

"Where are they?" he said, disappointed, as Alex and Olivia came running up behind him.

"They've gone out," Geneviève called from the kitchen. Sébastien, Alex, and Olivia went back in and saw a note that had been propped on the counter.

WENT WITH GRANDMA TO MEET AUNT MEG AND
UNCLE TONY AT THE FERRY. BACK SUPPERTIME-ISH.

LOVE,

MOM AND CHARLIE

Sébastien groaned. "They'd be so excited."

"But this way we can find the deed and surprise them when they get back," Claire said.

"True. Oh, won't Grandma be thrilled?"

"Let's do it!" Alex said.

The cousins assembled all the objects on the kitchen table.

"Grandpa said to use them in numbered order," Olivia said.

Geneviève pointed to the map. "That's number 1."

"What's number 2?" Sébastien said.

"The paintbrush," Olivia said, and grabbed it.

That didn't present any ideas.

"Number 3?" Claire asked.

"The vinegar," said Alex.

"Oh, I get it!" Olivia said. It must be an invisible map, and we have to paint it with vinegar to reveal the ink," she explained. She poured some vinegar into a bowl, then picked up the paintbrush. "Who wants to do the honors?"

"You do it, Liv. You're the artist," Alex said.

She dipped the brush in the vinegar and swept it across the top of the paper, just below the word MAP. The tangy smell of vinegar rose from the paper. Lines began to appear, squares and rectangles.

"Let's all take a turn," she said, handing the brush to her brother.

Alex swept the brush below where Olivia had painted. More squares and rectangles emerged. The brush went around the table. More lines appeared. All of the squares and rect-angles seemed to be enclosed in one larger rectangle.

"It's a diagram," Alex said. "A floor plan."

"It's the cottage!" Sébastien said. "Look, here's the upstairs – that's Grandpa's study," he said, pointing at one square. "And that's Grandma's room." He pointed at the square next to it.

"You're right, Seb," Geneviève said excitedly. "Look, this is the downstairs, and there's the studio . . . and the bathroom."

"And the kitchen," Claire said, painting the lower right corner of the page with vinegar. She handed the brush to Sébastien, who brushed over the final part of the map, the lower left.

"That's the living room, and look –" he said, as a mark appeared, " – an X! That must be where the deed is!"

The x appeared in a rectangular box marked on the wall facing the beach. "What's that?" Alex said, pointing to it.

"I don't know," Geneviève said. "Let's go find out!"

Grabbing the other objects, they dashed into the living room. Using the map to orient themselves, they figured out that the rectangle had to be the cupboard beneath the bay window.

Olivia opened the doors.

"The old wall!" Claire said. "Of course Grandpa would hide the deed here."

"But where?" Alex said, kneeling down and peering at the old wooden boards. "There's just boards here. I don't see any papers or anything."

"What's number 4?" Sébastien asked.

"The flashlight," Claire answered. She turned it on and shone the beam over the weathered boards. At first they appeared entirely blank.

Then Sébastien noticed something. "What's that?"

"What's what?" Alex said.

"That." Sébastien pointed to a tiny darkened area, about the size of a pea, in the middle board, about halfway up from the floor. "I can't tell what it is, but I think there's something there."

"I don't see anything," Olivia said.

"Me neither," Alex said. He adjusted his glasses. "Wait — there is something. But I can't make it out."

"What's next?" Claire asked.

"The prism," Geneviève said. She held it up, letting it dangle from the fishing line. "What do I do with it?"

"Try holding it in front of the flashlight," Sébastien said.

She did, and instantly a beam of light shot onto the wall. The beam skittered over the wall's surface as the prism rotated.

"Hold it still, Gen," Alex said.

Geneviève touched a fingertip to the prism and it slowly stopped turning. The beam of light settled on the dark spot, revealing a tiny metal coil embedded in the wall.

"What is it?" Alex said.

Geneviève leaned as close as she could without bumping the prism. "A spring of some kind," she said in a puzzled voice.

"This is crazy!" Olivia said with a laugh. "What's next?"

"The knitting needle," Sébastien said, grabbing it. "What do I do with it?"

"Try poking it at the spring and see what happens," Geneviève said.

Sébastien stuck the tip of the knitting needle into the center of the spring and pushed. The spring popped out. And then the board slid a fraction of an inch to the left.

"Oh my God!" Alex said. "Did that board just move?"

"It's a secret panel!" Geneviève said.

"Yikes!" Claire said. "What could be behind there? I hope . . . it's not a ghost or something."

"Don't be silly, Claire," Sébastien said, though he, too, half-expected something scary to pop out.

"Open it, open it!" Olivia said.

Sébastien wedged his finger into the narrow space and pushed. With a faint groan, the board slid a couple of inches farther to the left, fitting smoothly behind the one beside it. Behind it, a dark cavity loomed. It was about six inches deep.

An empty space stared back at them.

"Now what?" Alex asked. "There's got to be something in here. Let's have the flashlight."

Claire shone the light into the cavity. And there, sitting at the bottom of the empty space, was a wooden box.

Everyone stopped and stared.

"Oh, my –" Claire said. "Could it be . . . ?"

Geneviève lifted out the box. It was covered in dust. She blew, and dust motes danced in the flashlight beam. She placed the box on the windowsill.

It was an ordinary looking box, about the size of a box of tissues, and made of light-colored wood. The top was hinged on one side; at the front, there was a small padlock threaded through a couple of metal loops.

"The key, the key!" Olivia shouted. "Number 7!"

Geneviève grabbed the key. It fit perfectly into the padlock. She unlocked it, twisted it out of the loops, raised the lid – and there, sitting on a bed of velvet, was a scrolled piece of paper tied with red ribbon.

Geneviève lifted it out and untied the ribbon.

No one breathed.

Slowly, carefully, Geneviève unrolled the scroll of paper.

DEED IN TITLE
This certifies that the property located at
kilometer 12, South Waterfront Road,
Otter Island, British Columbia, has been duly registered
and recorded to the ownership of . . .

"We did it!"
"We found it! Woo-hoo!"

Alex burst into tears. Sébastien and Claire jumped around, pumping their fists in the air. Geneviève and Olivia hugged one another.

Just then they heard the sound of footsteps and voices. They dashed into the kitchen.

"Grandma, guess what!"

"You won't believe it!"

"Mom! Dad!" Alex yelled, running toward his parents.

"Grandma, we found –"

"Children!" Grandma ran toward them, her arms outstretched. "I remembered! Just this minute it came to me, what Sam said. It's in the old wall!"

The cousins burst out laughing. "We know, Grandma, we found it."

"Just now!"

The adults stood there, looking dumbfounded.

"You did? How?" Uncle Tony said.

"With the clues," Olivia said. "Claire squeezed into the cave and got the map –"

"Claire!" Eve said sharply. "What on earth –"

"Don't worry, Mom, it was fine. Only, we couldn't read the map –"

"'Cause Grandpa had made it with invisible ink," Alex said.

"So we had to paint it with vinegar –" Olivia said

"And we found the cupboard . . . and used the flashlight and the prism," Alex said.

"We poked with the knitting needle," Sébastien put in, "and the old wall moved! So we got the box and used the key –"

"And there was the deed –" Claire said.

"And here it is!" Geneviève unscrolled it.

Grandma burst out crying. Everybody started jumping around and laughing and hugging and shouting.

Finally, Grandma wiped her eyes. She held out her arms. "Come here, all of you."

The five cousins piled in for a hug.

Grandma sniffled again, then grinned, holding the deed to her chest. "They found it, Sam!"

TWENTY-TWO

CRY UNCLE

Ten minutes later, the entire family was crowded into a couple of booths at Tillie's Café, having ice cream sodas to celebrate. "And I don't even care that it's suppertime!" Eve said.

As soon as Grandma told Tillie the good news, she phoned Leon, and he came running in, followed by Bernie, whom Leon had called. Soon the café was filled with friends and neighbors, congratulating Grandma and forcing the children to tell the story of the discovery over and over again.

"Hidden in a cave?" Rachel said in disbelief.

"A spring released by a knitting needle?" Chad said.

"That Sam," Bernie said, wiping his eyes.

Grandma beamed.

———

Sébastien watched Charlie in disgust. Charlie was smiling and laughing along with everyone else. He'd hugged Grandma and Eve, back at the house, as if he couldn't be happier about the discovery of the deed. He'd even told the kids they'd done a great job.

What an actor! He had them all convinced.

That only made him an even bigger rat.

———

Finally, everyone finished their sodas and drifted outside. Grandma and Eve headed over to Muriel's store to tell her the good news. Aunt Meg and Uncle Tony went to pick up some groceries. Everyone arranged to meet at the cars in ten minutes.

Geneviève strolled down the street and sat on a bench. Leaning back, she closed her eyes and let the late afternoon sun warm her face. Nearby, she could hear Olivia and Sébastien laughing about something.

What a day! First the disastrous visit from Tantalus, then Osprey Cove, and finally the deed. From the lowest low to the highest high. Wait till she told Shane, she thought. He'd be so happy for Grandma.

As if thinking of him had conjured him up, Geneviève heard his voice.

"It's not my fault," Shane was saying.

Geneviève opened her eyes and sat up. She hadn't seen him in a few days. A shiver of excitement ran up her back. Where was he? His voice seemed to be coming from the other side of some hedges.

"You blew it. You didn't move fast enough," another voice said.

Geneviève recognized it. Stan Wilensky. Shane's uncle. She'd managed not to think about that for the last several days. Because it didn't necessarily mean anything. Even now. What could be more natural than a nephew and an uncle having a conversation?

She missed Shane's reply. Then Wilensky said sarcastically,

"Guess you're not as hot as you thought you were."

"I did my best!" Shane said irritably.

What?

"Well, it obviously wasn't good enough."

"What do you know about it?" Shane said with a chuckle. "Don't worry, she's crazy about me."

The blood rushed to Geneviève's face.

"A fat lot of good that does us now," Wilensky replied. "Our chance is gone."

"I'll still have that job in the new surf shop, right?"

"Not anymore."

Shane's voice turned surly. "You promised!"

"Only if you delivered," Wilensky said.

"But Uncle Stan —"

"You knew what you had to do. You blew it."

"But —"

"Too bad. No deed, no job."

Footsteps marched away. With a cry, Geneviève sprang up from the bench and ran to the car. She threw herself onto the backseat and burst into tears. *Lying scumbag! Working for his uncle the whole time. For the promise of a freaking job!* And she had been totally, completely, utterly taken in.

The humiliation. The heartbreak.

Pushing her face into the car seat, she sobbed.

A quiet footstep sounded beside the open car door. Without looking, Geneviève knew it was Sébastien. And she knew he must have heard.

Angrily she pushed herself up and wiped her face with her arm. Not looking at him, she said, "Go ahead. Rub it in."

Silence.

"You were right. I –" A sob escaped. " – was wrong."

Still, silence.

Geneviève turned. There was a strange look on Sébastien's face. Not gloating. Not pity. He was just looking at her.

He shook his head. Then he said softly, "Gen . . . I'm sorry."

Geneviève did something she never thought she'd do. She hurled herself into her brother's arms and cried on his shoulder.

TWENTY-THREE

FIVE BY FIVE BY FIVE . . .

Back at Grandma's, everyone was in the kitchen. Alex remembered they'd gathered like this on the first day they'd come. How different things were now! Back then, Grandma was in tears, terrified of losing her cottage. Now everyone was laughing, relieved that the cottage was saved.

Then Alex noticed that that wasn't true. Grandma wasn't laughing. She was sitting there, brooding, chin in hand, shoulders slumped.

"Grandma, what's the matter?" he asked.

Grandma looked at him. "Well, sweetheart, I'm overjoyed that I won't lose my home. But . . ." She sighed. "What's it going to be like? I'll have that blasted road going right by, trucks roaring up and down, dust and dirt and noise, Lookout Hill will be destroyed . . . . It won't be the same."

Silence fell.

"Maybe it won't be so bad, Mom," Eve began, but Uncle Tony interrupted.

"She's right, Eve," he said. "There's no sugar-coating the situation. It's going to be awful."

"If there were only some way to stop the mine," Aunt Meg said. "Some way to stop Tantalus from getting the permit."

"But how?" Grandma said. "They've done all the reports.

It's just a matter of time until the government gives them the go-ahead."

"Maybe they've slipped up somewhere," Eve said. "Maybe a lawyer could go over their submission, find something they missed. Then the government would have to turn them down."

Aunt Meg perked up. "Do we know any lawyers?"

As the conversation continued, Sébastien slipped out of the kitchen and went upstairs. He needed to do something, and the only thing he could think of was to go back to that slip of paper. Someone had sent it to Ted for a reason. It held some kind of message, maybe even a warning. Sébastien was sure of it. If only he could figure out what it was, maybe he could stop Tantalus from getting the permit.

Ridiculous! he told himself, turning on Grandpa's computer. As if he, an eleven-year-old kid, was going to find something that would stop the mine!

But he had to try.

While he waited for the computer to boot up, he drummed his fingers on the desk, thinking. So far he'd gotten nowhere trying to figure out a cipher that substituted or recombined letters. And the code clearly didn't use symbols or numbers.

Maybe, he thought, staring at the paragraph, the bolding itself was the key.

Worth a try. He typed SECRET CODES BOLD TYPEFACES into the search engine, and up popped a link for something called Bacon's Cipher.

Probably a waste of time, Sébastien thought, but he opened it anyway.

Bacon's Cipher, he read, used two different typefaces, such as two different fonts, or plain and bold letters, or plain and italic letters, to give each letter of the alphabet a five-character code.

Plain and bold, Sébastien thought. Sounded promising.

The pattern for each letter was spelled out in a key, where the number 1 stood for plain type and the number 2 stood for bold type.

a 11111	g 11221	n 12211	t 21121
b 11112	h 11222	o 12212	u-v 21122
c 11121	i-j 12111	p 12221	w 21211
d 11122	k 12112	q 12222	x 21212
e 11211	l 12121	r 21111	y 21221
f 11212	m 12122	s 21112	z 21222

So, for example, the code for the letter E was 11211, or plain-plain-bold-plain-plain, and the code for the letter L was 12121, or plain-bold-plain-bold-plain.

However many letters in the word you wanted to hide, Sébastien read, the fake message had to have five times as many letters. It didn't matter what the letters were, as long as there were five times as many as in the real word. Then, dividing the fake letters into groups of five, you used plain and bold typefaces to encode the real letters.

So, if the real word was DOG, with three letters, you needed a fake message with fifteen letters. Like:

Chocolate is good

Then you grouped the letters into chunks of five and used the plain and bold patterns in the key to encode the real letters:

D   O   G

Choco   **latei**   **sgoo**d

To decode the message, you divided the letters in the fake message into chunks of five and then used the key to figure out which letters they represented. So, to decode CHOCO, you looked in the key for the pattern plain-plain-plain-bold-bold, or 11122, and found that that was the pattern for the letter D. To decode LATEI, you looked for the pattern plain-bold-bold-plain-bold, or 12212, and found that that was the pattern for the letter O. To decode SGOOD, you looked for the pattern plain-plain-bold-bold-plain, or 11221, and discovered that it was the letter G.

D-O-G.

Seb's pulse began to race. He wasn't sure if this was the system used in the weird paragraph, but it sounded like it.

Quickly he copied the paragraph from the booklet:

The Otter **Island** tantalu**m** **m**ine **is green! It** **w**ill **be great** for th**e** envir**o**nment! Full **s**peed a**head** on th**is** exci**t**ing **mine** pro**j**ect **t**hat **promises** fantas**t**ic **profits** wh**i**le **p**rotecting fish, **b**ir**d**s, and **wild**life!

Then he rewrote the paragraph, dividing the letters into chunks of five:

The Ot	ter **Is**	land t	antal	**um min**	e **is gr**
een! **It**	**will b**	e **grea**	t for t	he env	ironm
ent! Fu	ll **spe**	ed **ahe**	ad on t	his ex	citin
g **mine**	proje	ct tha	t **prom**	ises f	antas
tic **pr**	ofits	while	**prote**	cting	fish,**b**
irds,a	nd **wil**	**d**life!			

It divided evenly into fives!

Okay, he said to himself, the first five-letter chunk is The Ot, and it has a pattern of plain-plain-plain-plain-plain, or 11111. He scanned the key and easily found that the letter with that pattern was A. He wrote A on a separate sheet of paper.

The next chunk was ter Is, and it had a pattern of bold-plain-plain-bold-plain, or 21121. That was the code for T.

A — T .

Seb's heart began to beat faster.

Next came land t: plain-bold-plain-bold-plain. 12121. L.

A — T — L.

He worked faster.

Next: antal: plain-plain-plain-plain-plain. 11111. Another A.

A — T — L — A.

Sébastien continued going back and forth between the groups of five letters and the key. Letter by letter, the word emerged.

A — T — L — A — N — T — U — S.

Atlantus? What on earth did that mean? Sébastien had heard of the mysterious continent of Atlantis – it was supposed to have disappeared under the ocean, wasn't it? But Atlantus?

Well, at least he had the first word. Back to work.

e grea: plain-bold-plain-bold-bold. 12122. M.

t for t: plain-bold-plain-plain-plain. 12111. I.

he env: plain-bold-bold-plain-plain. 12211. N.

ironm: plain-plain-bold-plain-plain. 11211. E.

M — I — N — E.

ATLANTUS MINE.

Sébastien scratched his head. He knew what a mine was, but what was an Atlantus mine?

He continued decoding the groups of five letters. The next part of the message said ENVIRONMENTAL.

ATLANTUS MINE ENVIRONMENTAL . . .

Back to work.

o**fits**: plain-plain-plain-bold-bold. 11122. D.

w**h**ile: plain-bold-plain-plain-plain. 12111. I.

prote: bold-plain-plain-plain-bold. 21112. S.

cting: plain-plain-plain-plain-plain. 11111. A.

fish **b**: bold-plain-plain-plain-bold. 21112. S.

D — I — S — A — S—

Sébastien's pulse began to race. Was this word going to say what he thought it was?

i**rds** a: bold-plain-plain-bold-plain. 21121. T.

nd **w**il: plain-plain-bold-plain-plain. 11211. E.

dlife!: bold-plain-plain-plain-plain. 21111. R.

D — I — S — A — S — T — E — R.

ATLANTUS MINE ENVIRONMENTAL DISASTER.

Sébastien gave a whoop of triumph. He'd done it! He'd cracked the code! Good old Bacon's Cipher! It had been tough, mind-numbingly tough, but whoever had written the message hadn't been able to get the secret past him. He grinned, thinking about how Grandpa would have relished the game, putting his head together with Sébastien's to solve the mystery.

Then confusion filled him as he gazed at the words again. What did they mean? What was the Atlantus mine, and why was it an environmental disaster? Why had someone written those words in secret code and sent them to Ted?

Quickly he typed "Atlantus mine environmental disaster" into the computer's search engine. Up popped a link titled ATLANTUS MINE: ENVIRONMENTAL REPORT. Puzzled, he clicked on it. A scientific-looking report filled the screen. It was written by Dr. Sophie Kalamas and Dr. Mohinder Dhillon.

Who were they?

Sébastien started scrolling through the report. Right on the first page, it said, "We hereby present the environmental assessment of the proposed Otter Island tantalum mine."

Otter Island?

He kept reading. The report described the island. It talked about Lookout Hill, Seal Bay, and Osprey Cove. It talked about the ferry dock and the public beach. It was *his* Otter Island, there was no doubt about it.

Phrases started leaping out: "Contamination of ground water." "Impacts to fish stocks." "Destruction of habitat."

He scrolled further and came to a graph titled "Greenhouse Gas Emissions from Construction." From almost zero on the left side of the graph, the bars rose steadily as they moved to the right.

Finally, he came to a page titled "Conclusions." In bold type it said, **"Our research leads to the conclusion that Atlantus Mining's proposed tantalum mine will have serious environmental impacts on Otter Island and should not proceed."**

Sébastien sat back. *Atlantus Mining's* tantalum mine?

He grabbed the OTTER ISLAND TANTALUM MINE: ENVIRONMENTAL REPORT he'd stolen from Wilensky Air and flipped through the pages. This report said the opposite from the one on his computer screen. It said that the mine would not have serious environmental impacts and that Tantalus Mining had plans to deal with any small problems that might arise.

What was going on here? He couldn't figure it out, though

he had a strong feeling there was something shady about it.

What should he do?

Tell somebody. But who? Grandma? Mom? Ch–

Charlie!

Sébastien gasped. Whatever this Atlantus Mining business was about, Charlie must be mixed up in it, just like he was mixed up with Tantalus Mining. Sébastien's stomach turned over at the thought that his mother's boyfriend, who acted like he loved her so much, was going to betray her in such a horrible way.

Who could Sébastien talk to?

Ted! Ted Crombie! The message had been intended for him. Sébastien had to show him what it said.

Would Ted believe him? Ted had been getting information from Tantalus. He had been writing articles in favor of the mine. He might not take the message seriously.

Sébastien knew he had to try anyway. Stuffing the sheet with the decoded message in his pocket, he ran outside and hopped on his bike.

TWENTY-FOUR

WHICH SIDE ARE YOU ON?

Sébastien dropped his bike on the grass outside the *Otter Observer* office and dashed inside. A receptionist sat at a desk, typing at a computer.

"Ted . . . Crombie . . . ," Seb panted.

"I'm sorry, Ted is with someone. Would you take a seat, please?"

"It's really important," Seb said, wiping his arm across his forehead.

The woman looked at him as if she didn't believe that a kid could have anything that important to tell a newspaper reporter. "He'll be with you as soon as he's free." She turned back to her computer.

Impatiently, Sébastien turned to sit down, but then he heard a familiar voice coming from down the hall – the last voice he wanted to hear right now. He darted past the receptionist's desk.

"Hey!" the woman shouted. "You can't do that!"

Ignoring her, Sébastien ran in the direction of the voice. He passed a couple of empty offices, jerked open a closed door to find a man on the phone with his feet on a desk, then came to a half-open door with CROMBIE on it. Seb pushed it open. There, behind a desk, sat Ted Crombie, and across from him – Charlie.

"I'm telling you, Ted, you have to get on it right away," Charlie was saying.

Get on it right away. He was telling Ted to write another positive story about the mine!

"Don't listen to him, Ted!" Sébastien shouted.

"What!" Ted gaped.

"Sébastien! What are you doing here?" Charlie said, turning pink.

Heels clacked down the hall. The receptionist poked her head in. "I'm sorry, Ted, I told him you were busy –"

"It's all right, Helen. Thanks."

With a baleful look at Sébastien, she left.

Sébastien turned back to Ted. "Don't believe a word he says, Ted. He's in with them!"

"Who's in with whom?" Ted said, looking baffled.

"What are you talking about?" Charlie said.

"You. And Tantalus. *And* Atlantus," Sébastien said with clear disgust.

"Who?" Charlie asked.

Sébastien rolled his eyes. "Nice try, Charlie."

"Excuse me, you two," Ted said, "but would someone mind telling me what's going on here?"

Charlie looked baffled, as if he had no idea what Sébastien was talking about. *Still acting,* Seb thought. Then, *Okay, Charlie, have it your way.*

He sat down and pulled the slip of paper out of his pocket. "Remember this?" he said to Ted.

Ted nodded. "Yeah. So?"

"What's that?" Charlie said, craning over Sébastien's shoulder.

"Like you don't know," Sébastien said sarcastically.

"Sébastien, I keep telling you –"

Sébastien told Ted the whole story. How he'd suspected something was funny about the slip of paper. How he became convinced that the bold and plain letters hid some kind of secret. How he'd tried, over and over, to break the code. And how, finally–

He whipped the other sheet out of his pocket.

Charlie drew his chair closer. Sébastien could feel him trembling. *Nervous about having the truth come out,* he thought.

"So finally I found this thing called Bacon's Cipher," Sébastien said. "It was really hard, but I figured it out. The weird paragraph is a false message. What it really says is –"

He unfolded the paper, and Ted read it aloud. "Atlantus mine environmental disaster."

Sébastien waited for Charlie to cringe or turn red or say, "No way!" Instead, Charlie looked . . . intrigued.

Huh? What's going on?

"What does it mean?" Ted asked.

"I don't know, but I found something else," Sébastien said and told Ted about the Atlantus Mining environmental report. Ted brought it up on his computer screen, and Charlie leaned close while Sébastien showed Ted the names of the two authors.

"Who the heck are Dr. Sophie Kalamas and Dr. Mohinder Dhillon?" Ted asked.

"I don't know," Sebastien said.

"It's a different environmental report," Charlie said slowly. He shot up straight. "Wait! There must be something funny about the other report – the Tantalus Mining one."

That was what *he* was starting to think, Sébastien thought. Why was Charlie saying it? And why was he looking excited?

A distinctly uncomfortable feeling began to grow in him.

"That's crazy," Ted said. "They're two separate reports. Two different companies. It must be some other mine."

"No," Sébastien said. "It's *our* mine." He showed them where the report talked about Otter Island.

"But it can't be —" Ted broke off as Sébastien showed him where the report listed all the environmental impacts the mine would have. Then Sébastien had Ted scroll down to the last page.

"**'Our research leads to the conclusion that Atlantus Mining's proposed tantalum mine will have serious environmental impacts on Otter Island and should not proceed,'**" Ted read aloud. He shook his head. "Who is Atlantus Mining, and why is this report talking about the Tantalus Mining mine?"

"I don't know," Sébastien began, "but it must be something shady —"

"Look!" Charlie interrupted. "Atlantus has all the same letters as Tantalus. — you just have to scramble them!"

"Whoa —" Sébastien said, suddenly getting what Charlie was saying.

But why is Charlie saying that? Isn't he on their *side?*

"They must have changed their name!" Charlie said.

"Now you've really gone off the deep end," Ted said.

But Charlie could be right, Sébastien thought with excitement. *In fact, it's the only thing that makes sense.*

"How can we find out?" Charlie said impatiently. "Ted, is there a Web site that lists companies?"

"Yes," Ted said, "but . . ." He tapped the keys, and a business site opened with a long list of names. Ted scrolled down.

There was no Atlantus Mining.

"Try Tantalus," Charlie suggested.

Ted scrolled farther.

TANTALUS MINING (FORMERLY KNOWN AS ATLANTUS MINING), said the listing.

The three of them stared at one another.

"The company was originally called Atlantus Mining . . ." Sébastien thought aloud.

"And they hired – who was it?" Charlie asked.

"Dr. Sophie Kalamas and Dr. Mohinder Dhillon," Sébastien answered.

"Right. They hired them to do the environmental assessment . . ."

"And they discovered that the mine was going to be an environmental disaster . . ." Sébastien went on, his mind racing.

"And Saxby and those guys knew they couldn't go public with that – because it would be the end of the mine – so they changed the name of the company," Charlie put in.

"And then they changed the report." Sébastien thought for a moment. Then it hit him. "Wayne Cheng must have changed it!"

"But that's nuts," Ted said. He lifted the OTTER ISLAND TANTALUM MINE: ENVIRONMENTAL REPORT. "Dr. Wayne Cheng is an eminent scientist."

"It's the only thing that fits," Sébastien said.

"No wonder he always looked so uptight," Charlie added.

Sébastien thought of something. He tapped a key and brought the screen back to the Atlantus Mining report. It was dated in January. Then he held up the OTTER ISLAND

TANTALUM MINE: ENVIRONMENTAL REPORT. April.

"See?" he said.

To Sébastien's amazement, Charlie threw his arms around him. "Sébastien! You're brilliant!"

"W-what?" Sébastien threw Charlie's arms off and gaped at him.

"First you figured out the secret code, and then you found the real report, and then you figured out what they were really up to. You're amazing!"

Sébastien was beginning to think he'd made a terrible mistake about Charlie.

Ted leaned back in his seat. "It's crazy. It's preposterous. But it looks like that's what happened." He sat back up and pounded his fist on the desk. "And after that Valerie London woman fed me all this information about how great the mine was!"

"Imagine the deception," Charlie said, shaking his head. "Fudging the numbers, changing the conclusions. What crooks!"

Ted's face turned red. "They hoodwinked me – and I fell for it."

"You certainly weren't the only one, Ted. Lots of people did. All those people who sold their land to Tantalus. All those people who invested in the mine. All those people who believed the mine would be good for Otter Island," Charlie said. "But that's not what's important now. What's important now is to get the word out – before Tantalus gets the permit."

"But if Tantalus handed in a fake environmental report, the government won't give them the permit, will they?"

Sébastien said. "Won't the mine be dead?"

"I'd certainly think so," Charlie replied. "But I'd still feel a whole lot better if Ted exposed the whole thing right away."

"Oh, you can believe I'll do that," Ted said grimly. "And you'll read all about it in the *Otter Observer.*"

"Good," Charlie and Sébastien said together.

Ted lifted the slip of paper. "But who sent this to me?"

Charlie shrugged. "Maybe it was Dr. Kalamas and Dr. Dhillon. Maybe they found out what Tantalus had done and they had to let someone know – without Tantalus finding out they were doing it."

"Or maybe it was Wayne Cheng," Sébastien said. "Maybe he had a guilty conscience."

Ted shook his head. "To think that I would have missed the whole thing if it hadn't been for you, Sébastien. You did an amazing job!" He shook Sébastien's hand. "I'll tell you one thing. You've got a future as an investigative reporter – or a secret agent."

—●—

Sébastien avoided looking at Charlie as he walked over to his bike. "Uh . . . Charlie . . ." he began, "I'm sorry . . ."

"Let me get this straight," Charlie said. "You guys thought I was in with them?"

"Yeah, but –"

"Sébastien!"

"But it looked like it!" Sébastien felt his cheeks grow warm. "We saw you with them . . . Saxby and Wilensky . . . down by Wilensky Air."

"I was just trying to string them along, to get them to

reveal what their plans really were."

"And we saw you looking at the report . . ."

"Trying to find a clue to prove there was something shady going on."

"And then you got a phone call from Wilensky . . ." he said lamely, knowing already that it had been perfectly innocent.

"About my float-plane reservation! For crying out loud, Sébastien, how could you kids think that about me?"

"Claire didn't," Seb admitted. "She wouldn't believe it."

"Good old Claire," Charlie said with a chuckle. "At least someone had faith in me."

Sébastien swallowed. "I'm really sorry, Charlie. I thought . . . I was wrong."

"Sébastien," Charlie said, "don't you know that I would never do anything to hurt your grandma? Or your mom? I love them both. I love this place."

Sébastien stared at the ground. He knew that now. If only he could curl up in a ball and disappear. If only he could go back in time and erase all those terrible things he'd said about Charlie.

He felt a hand on his shoulder. "Hey," Charlie said, and there was a smile on his face. "No hard feelings, Seb."

"Really?"

Charlie nodded. "Now that I think about it, I'm impressed that you were prepared to go to such lengths to protect your grandma – and your mom."

The knot in Sébastien's stomach eased a little. He climbed onto his bike seat.

"One more thing, Sébastien," Charlie said, lifting Sébastien's chin. "Your grandpa would be proud of you. Not just for cracking the code. For everything."

Sébastien felt tears rush to his eyes. Blinking them away, he said something he'd never expected to say.

"You too, Charlie."

TWENTY-FIVE

CELEBRATE!

"You mean . . . the mine is dead? Really dead?" Grandma's voice sounded disbelieving.

"Really and truly dead," Charlie said. He clamped a hand on Sébastien's shoulder. "And all because of your grandson here. If it hadn't been for Seb, Tantalus probably would have gotten away with it . . . and gotten the permit."

Eve hugged Sébastien. "Way to go, honey!"

Alex scratched his head. "I don't get it. Five times as many letters as what?"

"I'll show you later, Alex," Sébastien said.

Grandma wiped the tears from her eyes. "This calls for a celebration. A feast! In honor of Sam – and Sébastien."

"And the cottage," Aunt Meg said.

"And the end of that horrible mine," Uncle Tony added.

"Let's make all our favorites," Claire said. "All the recipes that led to the deed."

"Great idea," Grandma said. "I remember there was *Pesto* . . ."

"And *Painterman Eggs*," Olivia said.

"And *Zucchini Pickles*," Alex said.

"And *Osprey Cove Clam Pot* – for Grandpa," Geneviève said, "and *Chocolate Cinnamon Sparkle Cookies* for me."

"And *Muriel's Berry Pandowdy*," Sébastien added.

"And *Emergency Fudge!*" Claire shouted.

"As long as you don't get sick this time," Eve said, pulling one of Claire's pigtails.

"You knew about that?" Claire said, turning pink.

Everyone laughed.

"I notice," Aunt Meg said wryly, "that the menu is a bit heavy on the sweets."

"Don't blame us," Claire said, eyes wide and innocent. "Grandpa's the one who put the clues in those recipes."

"Right, it's all Sam's fault," Grandma said with a laugh. She opened her arms wide, and the cousins gathered in. "You children are great cooks – *and* great detectives. Say! We should call you the Teaspoon Detectives."

The cousins looked at one another and grinned.

"Cool!" Alex said.

Grandma released them and rolled up her sleeves. "Come on then, you wonderful Teaspoon Detectives – let's get cooking!"